"Sean, About That Kiss..."

Yeah, it was pretty much uppermost in his mind at the moment. Damn, he hadn't reacted that fast to any other woman before.

"It was a good one," he admitted.

If he had his way, he'd be taking his new bride upstairs to her suite. He'd lay her down on the closest flat surface he could find, then he'd hitch the skirts of her dress up and stare down into her eyes as he…

"We can't do that again," she said, effectively snapping him right out of his private fantasies.

"Sure we can," Sean countered, moving a little closer to her. "Kissing's not sex."

"It is the way *you* do it," she murmured.

His voice soft, his words careful, he said, "It was just a kiss, Melinda. It won't go anywhere else unless you want it to."

* * *

Dear Reader,

Writing these letters is sometimes hard and sometimes easy… This time, it's a snap!

The Temporary Mrs. King is Sean King's book, and frankly, I've been dying to write about him since he first showed up in his brother Rafe's book.

Sean is, to the outside world, an easygoing, laid-back kind of guy. He has a quick sense of humor, he's loyal to the bone and like every other King cousin, family is everything to him. But there's more to Sean than meets the eye. He's learned the hard way about betrayal, and the secret in his past haunts him still.

Melinda Stanford looks as though she has it all. She grew up with a doting grandfather on a small, privately owned Caribbean island. She's beautiful, smart and wealthy— or is she? Her doting grandfather is becoming more demanding lately, wanting to see his only grandchild settled and happy before he dies.

A bargain is struck, more secrets are born and a romance that made me smile all the way through it begins.

I really hope you enjoy Sean's book as much as I did.

Visit me at www.maureenchild.com and at www.facebook.com/maureenchild. You can also write to me at P.O. Box 1883, Westminster, CA 92684-1883.

Happy reading!

Maureen

MAUREEN CHILD

THE TEMPORARY MRS. KING

Recycling programs
for this product may
not exist in your area.

ISBN-13: 978-0-373-73138-1

THE TEMPORARY MRS. KING

Copyright © 2011 by Maureen Child

This edition published by arrangement with Harlequin Books S.A.

For questions and comments about the quality of this book please contact us at Customer_eCare@Harlequin.ca.

www.Harlequin.com

Printed in U.S.A.

Books by Maureen Child

Harlequin Desire

††*King's Million-Dollar Secret* #2083
One Night, Two Heirs #2096
††*Ready for King's Seduction* #2113
††*The Temporary Mrs. King* #2125

Silhouette Desire

†*Scorned by the Boss* #1816
†*Seduced by the Rich Man* #1820
†*Captured by the Billionaire* #1826
††*Bargaining for King's Baby* #1857
††*Marrying for King's Millions* #1862
††*Falling for King's Fortune* #1868
High-Society Secret Pregnancy #1879
Baby Bonanza #1893
An Officer and a Millionaire #1915
Seduced Into a Paper Marriage #1946
††*Conquering King's Heart* #1965
††*Claiming King's Baby* #1971
††*Wedding at King's Convenience* #1978
††*The Last Lone Wolf* #2011
Claiming Her Billion-Dollar Birthright #2024
††*Cinderella & the CEO* #2043
Under the Millionaire's Mistletoe #2056
   "The Wrong Brother"
Have Baby, Need Billionaire #2059

†Reasons for Revenge
††Kings of California

Other titles by this author available in ebook

MAUREEN CHILD

is a California native who loves to travel. Every chance they get, she and her husband are taking off on another research trip. The author of more than sixty books, Maureen loves a happy ending and still swears that she has the best job in the world. She lives in Southern California with her husband, two children and a golden retriever with delusions of grandeur. Visit Maureen's website, www.maureenchild.com.

To my mother-in-law, Mary Ann Child.
She raised five sons, so she knows all about
dealing with hardheaded men.

Thanks for everything, Mom. I love you.

One

"I think we should get married."

Sean King choked on his sip of beer. Slamming the icy bottle down onto the polished teak bar, he coughed until tears filled his eyes. He was forced to blink them away to see the woman who had nearly killed him with six little words.

She was worth it.

Her hair was nearly as black as his. Her eyes were a softer blue than his own and her skin was a pale honey color, telling him she spent a lot of time outdoors. She had high cheekbones, delicately arched black brows and a look of fierce determination stamped on her features.

Something inside him stirred when she licked her lips and, just for a second, he let his gaze drop to appreciate the rest of her. She was wearing a lemon-yellow sundress that showed off a pair of truly amazing legs. Her sandals boasted bright white flowers positioned over toes that were painted bloodred.

Finally lifting his gaze to hers, he gave her a half smile and said, "Married? Don't you think we should have dinner first?"

Her lips twitched briefly, then she shot a look at the bartender, as if assuring herself he was far enough away to not overhear her. "I know how strange that sounded...."

He laughed. "Strange is a good word for it."

"...*but*, I have my reasons."

"Good to know," he said and lifted his beer for another sip. "Bye now."

She blew out an exasperated breath. "You're Sean King. You're here to meet with Walter Stanford—"

Intrigued, Sean narrowed his eyes on her. "News travels fast on a small island."

"Even faster when Walter is your grandfather."

"Grandfather?" he repeated. "That means you're—"

"Melinda Stanford, yes," she finished for him, then glanced uneasily around again.

For the wealthy, pampered granddaughter of the man who owned this island, she seemed a little spooky.

"Look, would you mind if we took this to one of the tables? I'd really rather not be overheard."

He could guess why. Proposing to a man you'd never met before wasn't the most normal way of introducing yourself. Pretty, but she didn't seem to be playing with all of her marbles. She didn't wait for him to agree, just walked toward one of the half-dozen empty tables in the hotel bar.

Sean watched her, deliberating whether or not to follow her. Sure, she was gorgeous. But clearly she was a little unhinged, too.

She looked bright as a sunbeam sitting in the dark

corner of the once elegant and now tired-looking bar. Thirty years ago, this place was no doubt considered top-of-the-line. But it had seen its day come and go and hadn't tried hard enough to keep up.

Now, the wood floors had deep scars that several coats of polish couldn't disguise. The walls were in need of fresh paint and the windows were too small. There were some nice touches though. Sort of art deco, Sean thought. The throughways were rounded at the top, arched with clean lines, which he liked. Round mirrors with tiled edges. Rectangular tables with bowed legs and mosaic inlaid surfaces. The wall sconces were Tiffany-esque with a modernistic thirties sense of style. It was beautiful, but definitely needed a face-lift. If it were his place, Sean would have taken out the front wall entirely and replaced it with glass, affording the patrons a spectacular view of the ocean. And he'd have clung to the art deco style and added a stained glass window filled with sharp angles and curves over the door. The hazards of running a construction company, he supposed. He was forever remodeling places in his mind.

But this wasn't his bar and he had a beautiful, if a little weird, woman waiting on him. Since he wasn't meeting Walter Stanford until the next morning and he had a few hours to kill anyway…Sean smiled to himself as he walked toward her.

He took a seat opposite her and leaned back in his chair, stretching his legs out in front of him. Holding his bottle of beer atop his flat belly, he tipped his head to one side, and studied her quietly, waiting for her to explain. He didn't have to wait long.

"I know you're here to buy the land on the North Shore."

"Not exactly a secret," he said, taking another sip of the

icy beer. He took a quick look at the label. A local brew, it was exceptional. Once they got the go-ahead and Rico's hotel was up and running, he'd tell his cousin to stock this beer in the bar.

Shifting his gaze to her, Sean shrugged. "It's probably all over the island that the Kings are negotiating with your grandfather."

"Yes," she said, folding her hands together on the table-top. Somehow, she managed to look both prim and incredibly sexy. "Lucas King was here a couple of months ago. He didn't get very far with Grandfather."

Irritating, but true.

In fact, Sean himself had already had one phone conversation with Walter and it hadn't gone well. Which was the reason he was here, in person.

In the Caribbean, Tesoro was one of the smaller islands and privately owned. Walter Stanford was practically a feudal lord around here. He had his hand in most of the local businesses and guarded his island from newcomers like a pit bull at the end of a very short chain.

Sean's cousin Rico King was bound and determined to expand his hotel empire and he wanted to build an exclusive resort here. On Tesoro. King Construction—Sean and his half brothers Rafe and Lucas—would be partners in the deal. But it wasn't going to happen without that land. So for months, the Kings had been wheeling and dealing, trying to convince Stanford that a King hotel would mean great things for this island. New jobs, more tourists and plenty of money hitting local cash drawers.

Rico had been here himself to see the old man. Followed in quick succession by Sean's brothers Rafe and then Lucas. Now it was Sean's turn at bat, so to speak. He was the one sent in when things were looking bad. Sean's charm and laid-back attitude were usually all it took to cinch a deal. He knew how to play hardball. He just never let others in on that secret.

"I'm not Lucas," he said with confidence. "I'll get the deal with your grandfather."

"Don't count on it," she told him. "He's very stubborn."

"You don't know the Kings," he said. "We invented stubborn."

She sighed and leaned toward him. The deeply scooped neckline of her sundress dipped, giving him a peek at her full breasts and just the smallest hint of a lacy bra. Sean reluctantly shifted his gaze to hers when she started speaking again.

"If you really want the land, there's a sure way to get it."

He shook his head and chuckled. Yeah, she was gorgeous, but he wasn't in the market for a new woman in his life—let alone a *wife*. No, he'd complete this deal his way. And he wouldn't need Melinda Stanford to do it. Chuckling again, he said, "The only way to get the land is by marrying you."

"Exactly."

He frowned. "You're actually serious."

"Absolutely."

"Are you on medication?"

"Not yet," she muttered. Then louder, she said, "Look, my grandfather is on a campaign to see me married with babies at my feet."

Sean shuddered. Sure, his brothers and far too many of his cousins had been taking the marital plunge lately. Lucas just last year. But not Sean. Nope. Been there, done that, survived to tell the tale. Not that anyone in his family had ever heard about Sean's thankfully brief trip into marriage hell.

He wasn't about to get married again.

"Good luck with that," he said and started to get up.

She reached across the table and grabbed his hand.

Instantly, heat sizzled where their palms met. Sean's body responded to that heat in a blink. It caught him off guard, that flash of something…tantalizing. One look into her eyes told him she was as surprised as he was. And just as determined to ignore it. He could be attracted to a woman without doing anything about it. Hell, he hadn't been led around by his dick since he was nineteen.

Though…the heat was still there, so to avoid temptation, he pulled his hand free of her grip and told himself he didn't miss that sweep of heat.

"You could at least listen to me," she said.

Frowning now, Sean eased back down in his chair. Not that he was interested in what she had to say, but why take the risk of offending a member of the very family he'd come here to do business with? "Fine. Listening. Make it fast."

"Okay. Bottom line is, I want you to marry me."

"Yeah, I got that. Why?"

"It makes sense."

"In which universe?"

"You want the land for your cousin to build a hotel. I want a temporary husband."

"Temporary?"

She laughed shortly and the sound was rich and musical. She shook her head until her soft, black hair floated around her like a dark halo. "Of course temporary. Did you think I was proposing a lifetime deal? To a man I've never met?"

"Hey," he reminded her, "you're the one proposing before I even knew your name, so watch the insults."

"Fine." She nodded, serious again. "Here's the deal.

When you meet with my grandfather, he's going to suggest a merger/marriage."

"How do you know?"

She waved one hand. "Because he's already tried at least four times."

"He didn't try this with Lucas or Rafe."

"Because they're *already* married."

"Ah. Right." Why was he trying to make sense of a situation that was clearly nuts?

"Anyway," she continued, "my grandfather will offer to sell you the land if you marry me. All I'm asking is that you accept."

"And marry you."

"Temporarily."

"How long is temporarily?" He couldn't even believe he was asking the question. He didn't want a wife, temporary or not. All he wanted to do was buy the land.

She frowned a little and tapped the tip of her finger against her chin while she thought about it. "Two months should be enough," she finally said with a nod. "Grandfather believes that even a business deal marriage could become something real given enough time. I don't."

"Right there with ya," Sean said, tipping his beer bottle at her in salute.

"My point is, if we're married two months, then Grandfather will think we've given it a try and it just didn't work out. Long enough to soothe him and short enough that neither of us should mind too much."

"Uh-huh." He looked at her, wondering how this day had gone from normal into the world of weird. "And you've chosen *me* for the honor of temporary husband... why?"

She sat back in her chair and drummed her fingertips

on the table. She might look cool and composed, Sean told himself, but her nerves were showing anyway.

"I did some research into you."

"What?"

"Well," she explained, "I'm not about to marry just anybody."

"Oh yeah," he said nodding, "I can see that."

"You were a good student in college, majored in computer sciences. You graduated and went into business with two of your half brothers. You're the tech guy, but also the one they call on to make the hard sell." She took a breath and Sean just stared at her. "You live in a rehabbed water tower in Sunset Beach California and you love your sister-in-law's cookies."

He frowned and took a long drink of his beer. Sean didn't much care for being researched. And he really didn't care for what she had to say next.

"You don't do commitment," she said, still tapping her fingers on the tabletop. "You're a serial monogamist—one woman only until you move on to the next one. Your exes all speak highly of you though, so that tells me you're a nice enough guy despite the fact that you can't maintain a relationship."

"Excuse me?"

"The longest relationship you had was in college. That lasted nearly nine months, though I couldn't find out what happened to end it—"

And she never would, Sean thought, deciding he'd had enough. Beautiful or not, she was starting to annoy him.

"That's it. I'm done." He leaned across the table and stared into those beautiful, sea-blue eyes of hers and said, "I'll get the land and I'll do it my way. I'm not interested in your schemes, babe, so try them on somebody else."

"Wait. Just…wait." She gave him a wide-eyed look out

of those beautiful blue eyes and he felt himself weakening. "This is coming out all wrong and I know it. I'm sorry if I offended you."

"Not offended," he assured her. "Just not interested."

Melinda felt a quick jolt of something like panic. She'd completely messed this up and she didn't want to risk having him turn her down. So she took a long breath and said, "Just, give me a chance to start over, okay?"

He gave her a wary look, but he didn't stand up and walk out, so she took that as a good sign.

God, where should she start? Funny, but she'd been planning on ambushing Sean King since she'd first heard about his upcoming visit weeks ago. Hence the research, she thought wryly. But in all that time, she'd never really considered how she was going to explain all of this without sounding like a complete loon.

"Okay, let me back up a little. The thing is, I'll come into a trust fund once I get married. With that, I can live my own life. Don't get me wrong here. I love my grandfather. He's a sweetie. But," she added with a helpless shake of her head, "he's really old school. He thinks women need to be married and having babies. Period. And he's relentless in trying to find a husband for me. I just thought, if I could get one on my own terms…"

"Okay," he said. "I get that. I guess what I'm wondering is again, why me?"

"Because this benefits both of us," she said, warming to her subject. At least he was listening. "You get the land. I'll get the trust fund, and then we'll both get a divorce."

He scowled a little, still unconvinced, so Melinda took a wild shot. "I could…pay you for your time…."

Instantly, anger flared in his eyes. "I'm not going to have you pay me to marry you. I don't need your money."

That reaction told her she'd made the right choice. Heaven knew there were millions of men who would have been more than happy to take her money. But Sean King was so wealthy in his own right, her trust fund, though immense to her, was probably nothing more than spending money to him.

Still, it spoke to his character that he was offended at the idea of her buying his services.

"Okay, but you and your cousin do want to build a hotel on Tesoro?"

"Yeah," he said.

"And to do that, you need the land."

"Yeah."

"To get the land, you'll need *me*." When he didn't look convinced, she said, "I know you don't believe me, but you should. You're meeting with Grandfather in the morning, aren't you?"

He nodded.

"Great. Then why don't we have dinner tonight? We can talk more about this and maybe I can convince you."

He gave her a slow smile that was hardly more than a slight curve of his mouth, but she felt the impact of it slam into her. Sean King oozed charm and sex appeal. The man was bristling with testosterone and Melinda felt a shiver of appreciation shoot through her.

Oh, this could get dangerous, she told herself.

"Dinner, huh?" He set his beer down and nodded. "Okay. I never turn down an opportunity for dinner with a beautiful woman. But I warn you, I'm not interested in being married."

"I know," she told him. "That's why you're perfect."

He shook his head and laughed. "I can't decide if you're crazy or not."

"Not crazy," she assured him. "Just determined."

"Beautiful and determined," he murmured. "A dangerous combination."

Heat flashed through her veins in spite of the fact that she didn't want to be attracted to him. She ignored the warmth still blossoming inside her and said, "There's a restaurant in town. Diego's. I'll meet you there at seven."

"I'm agreeing to dinner," he said with another half smile. "Not marriage." He stood up and looked down at her. "Diego's. Seven."

When he walked away, Melinda watched him. He was tall and lean and moved with a kind of lazy grace that men with lots of confidence seemed to adopt. Sean King was more than she'd expected.

She only hoped he wasn't more than she could handle.

"Lucas, what do you know about Melinda Stanford?" Sean spoke into his cell phone as he stood out on the end of the pier, watching the fishing boats head into the harbor.

"She's Walter's granddaughter."

"Yeah, I know that much."

"Well, what else is there?"

Way too much to go into over the phone, Sean thought. "Did you meet her when you were on Tesoro?"

"Briefly," Lucas said. "But then, my whole trip was brief. Walter said 'No' so fast, I didn't even get to unpack my bag before I was on the launch taking me back to civilization."

"Right." Sean nodded thoughtfully and kept his gaze fixed on the ocean.

"So what's this about?" Lucas asked. "Problem already? The great Sean charm not working?"

"In your dreams." Sean laughed, turned around and headed back down the dock. "I told you I'd get the land and I will."

"Yeah…good luck with the old man. I think he got a charm immunization."

"We'll see," Sean said.

Diego's was small and bright and popular with both locals and tourists. Seafood was the specialty and it was served at small, square tables decorated with brilliantly colored tablecloths that shone like jewels in the candlelit atmosphere. Patio dining offered more privacy, as there were fewer tables and those were spread far apart, but even the customers who stayed inside had a breathtaking view of the ocean and the pristine beach through a wide bank of windows. Moonlight glowed in the night sky and dazzled the water with silver light.

A sigh of a cool breeze slipped in off the ocean and danced around Melinda as she sat on the patio. Fall weather on Tesoro was capricious at best. Warm during the days, the nights could be cold or as it was tonight, almost sultry.

But then, Melinda thought, taking a slow sip of her ice-cold wine, maybe it wasn't the weather making her feel hot and uncomfortable. Maybe it was Sean King.

No, she told herself immediately. That couldn't be it. Because she refused to be attracted to him. She wasn't interested in a man and didn't think she ever would be again. This was strictly a business proposal and it would really be better for both of them if they could keep sexual heat out of the mix entirely.

Nerves skittered in her stomach. She trailed her fingertips up and down the stem of her wineglass and told herself that she was doing the right thing. The only thing.

She needed a husband.

Now all she had to do was convince Sean King that he was the man for the job.

"No pressure," she whispered.

She wasn't sure what caught her attention. The sound of leather soles scraping against the stone floor of the patio? Or was it something more elemental than that? Was it the feel of Sean King's gaze locked on her?

Whatever the reason, Melinda looked up to see the man walking toward her. His features were carefully blank, but for the half smile curving his mouth. He wore black slacks, a white, button-down shirt, open at the throat and a black jacket—and somehow, he managed to look both casual *and* dangerous.

Two

"Romantic setting for a business deal," Sean commented as he sat down opposite her.

Melinda took a long, deep breath and forced a smile she wasn't quite feeling. The nerves jumping inside her were now racing at a gallop. This was too important for her to make a mistake. Somehow, she had to convince Sean to marry her—temporarily.

"I wasn't going for romantic," she told him. "Just quiet."

"You got both," he said, nodding to the waiter when he stepped up to the table to pour wine. He waited until the server had moved off again before lifting his glass to take a small sip. Then he set the glass down, leaned his forearms on the tabletop and looked at her. Waiting again.

His gaze was steady and the expression on his face unreadable. Good sign? Bad sign? Melinda didn't know. But there was one sure way to find out.

"I'm really sorry I dumped all of this on you out of the blue this afternoon."

He shrugged. "No good way to propose to a stranger, I suppose."

"True." Shaking her head, Melinda said, "I know this all seems really strange, but you have to understand that my grandfather is very protective of me."

"So much so he tries to barter you off to business associates?" Sean quipped.

Melinda stiffened. *She* could complain about her grandfather all she wanted, but she wouldn't let someone else—especially someone who didn't even know him—take a shot at him. "He's trying to see me taken care of."

Sean leaned back in his chair and scraped one hand across the back of his neck. "And if you were a simpering maiden trapped in the middle ages, that would make sense."

This wasn't starting off very well, she told herself and then decided to ignore whatever comments he made. He didn't understand yet, that was all.

"Okay, yes," she agreed, "he's a little old-fashioned."

Both of his eyebrows arched.

"Fine. More than a little." She blew out a breath and explained. "I grew up here on Tesoro. My grandfather raised me when my parents died in a small plane crash when I was five."

He frowned at that, then took a sip of wine. Still not giving anything away. Not letting her get even a hint of what he might be thinking. He was probably an excellent poker player, Melinda told herself. She, on the other hand, was terrible at card games. She couldn't bluff to save her life. She was much more up-front and honest—well, she admitted silently, she wasn't exactly being honest with her grandfather in all of this. But then, she had tried to talk him out of this husband hunt he was on. Sadly, she hadn't been able to change his mind.

At the thought of Walter Stanford, she smiled in spite of her frustration. Her grandfather had been the one constant in her life. The one person who had always loved her no matter what. He was only trying to see her married because to *him*, that meant she would be protected and loved even when he was gone.

Which she so didn't want to think about. A world without Walter Stanford in it just didn't seem possible.

"Anyway," Melinda said, "he's getting older now and worrying about leaving me alone. I've told him that I'll be fine, but he comes from a generation that believed in taking care of women. I'm his only family and he wants to protect me." She gave him a long look. "You come from a big family and you're very close to your brothers. That's another reason why I'm coming to you with this plan. You understand family loyalties."

"I do," he admitted with a nod. "In fact, that's the one part of this whole thing that I totally get. I understand your grandfather's motivations. What I can't figure out is why you're willing to play along with his plans."

She smoothed her palms over the skirt of her cream-colored tank dress and tugged at the hem, but couldn't get it to reach the tops of her knees. "Because I love him. I don't want him to be worried…"

"…*And*?"

He was right, there was more. Quite a bit more.

"And, once I'm married, as I said, I'll come into my trust fund."

"Ah," he said, with a small smile. "And by marrying me, you don't have to worry about your new hubby making off with your money."

"Exactly." She returned that smile and felt a bit of her

nerves slide away. He was surprisingly easy to talk to once you got past the weirdness of the conversation.

"And again, how long would this marriage last?"

"I think two months should do it," she said, warming to her subject now that they were talking specifics. She had been working on this plan for weeks now and in her mind, at least, it all worked out perfectly. And so far so good. Sean King was still sitting opposite her. He hadn't said yes, *yet*. But, he hadn't walked out and he hadn't said no—precisely. "It's long enough that my grandfather would be convinced we at least tried to make it work."

"And once our marriage 'fails,' you think he'd stop trying to marry you off?"

"I think so," she said, chewing at her bottom lip as she considered it. "I *hope* so," she corrected after a minute or two. "But basically I'm tired of fending off men trying to buy my grandfather's goodwill. Besides, this is my only chance to get my trust fund *my* way. Well, mostly my way. I'll still be married, like Grandfather wants, but it will be a husband I choose and the kind of marriage I want."

He shifted in his chair and the breeze ruffled his black hair, lifting it off his forehead. He was still listening, so Melinda hurried on.

"Like I said earlier, if you agree, we'll get married and stay married for two months. I'll get my trust fund. You'll get your land. And then we'll *both* get a divorce."

The waiter showed up just then, so whatever Sean might have said would have to wait. Impatient now, sensing that just maybe he was beginning to come around, it seemed to take forever for them to order their meal. Finally, though, it was done, and they were alone again.

"So?" she asked. "What do you think?"

That was easily enough answered. Sean was still fairly sure she needed medication.

And yet…He draped one arm over the back of his chair and studied her.

Warm night, cold wine and a beautiful woman sitting across the table from him. In Sean's world, that sounded just about perfect. His gaze swept up and down Melinda Stanford, from the thick black waves of her hair to the blue-green stones glittering at her ears to the dip in the neckline of her dress, to the shine of her manicured nails. She was gorgeous. No doubt. But she was also complicated. And maybe crazy.

Still. Didn't mean he couldn't consider her proposal. In fact, he'd spent the last few hours doing just that.

Her grandfather, Walter Stanford, had shut down every deal the Kings had proposed over the last few months. Walter hadn't been interested, no matter how high their offers had gone. Either the old man seriously didn't need the money or he was as crazy as his granddaughter. But as soon as that thought entered his head, Sean discounted it. The old man wasn't a loon.

He was crafty.

Walter knew what he wanted and wasn't willing to settle for less. How the hell could a *King* of all people resent that? The King family did the same thing. They never took no for an answer and never gave up on something they wanted.

Sean smiled to realize that he and ol' Walter would probably get along great.

"What's so funny?"

"What?"

"You're smiling," she pointed out, managing to look both gorgeous and offended. "I asked what was so funny?"

She was insulted, Sean realized and he couldn't really blame her. No doubt she thought he was laughing silently at her well-presented offer. And as he considered the fact that it was *so* well-presented, he had to wonder if he was the first man to receive this weird proposal.

"How many times have you tried this?" he asked, leaning toward her so he could keep his voice down. Tables on the patio were few and the other diners sparse, but it paid to be careful.

She frowned slightly. "You're the first."

"Why? Why pick me?"

"I told you. I checked you out."

"Yes," he said, "but you'd already decided that I would be the lucky winner or you wouldn't have bothered doing your research."

She chewed at her bottom lip, and he wondered if it was nerves or just a habit. Then she reached for her wineglass and took a long sip. She set the glass down again before saying, "I knew my grandfather was talking to you. He kept me posted on the negotiations between him and your family. He told me that *you* had taken over from Lucas and not long after that I saw a picture of you, okay? And you looked...*nice*."

"Nice?" he repeated, appalled at the idea. "Old maid schoolteachers are 'nice.' Puppies are 'nice.' Ice cream on a hot day is 'nice.' *Men,* especially Kings, are not nice."

"Yeah," she muttered, "I'm getting that."

He'd never been called nice in his life. Funny. Handsome. Smart. And by some, he admitted, cold. Closed off. But never "nice." What picture of him could have possibly given her that impression?

"Where'd you see this photo?"

"It was in one of those celebrity magazines they sell at the grocery store." She flushed when she said it, almost as if embarrassed to admit she read the damn things. But millions did, Sean knew.

"You were at a football game with one of your brothers—"

Sean nodded. "Lucas," he provided, remembering that shot of him and his brother at a pre-season game. If his secretary hadn't shown it to him, he would have been unaware of it. He never paid attention to the photographers who were always ready to take pictures of the King family. It was just part of being who he was. Nodding, he said, "We hit the first pre-season game together every year."

"Well, in the picture, you were laughing and you looked friendly."

"Better than nice, but just barely," he admitted. He had an easygoing attitude to most of life, he supposed, which worked well in business, since his opponents were never ready for him to turn on them. But as far as women were concerned, most of those he knew would never think of describing him as nice, for God's sake.

Nice was...*nice*. He wasn't. Not at the heart of him. And usually it didn't take long for people to pick up on that.

She shrugged a little. "The point is, you looked like a man I could talk to about all of this. When I found out you were coming to Tesoro personally, I decided to take a stand."

"By lying to your grandfather."

"Not a lie," she argued quickly. "We actually *will* be married. So it's more of a colorful representation of the truth."

He fought back a smile. Seems Melinda Stanford had her own rules to play by. Well, Sean could admire anyone who set out to do something and didn't let anything get in the way. He could even take a step back and see that from her point of view, he actually *was* the perfect temporary husband. The question was, could he see it from his point of view?

Their dinner arrived before he could say anything else and, for a few minutes, they each focused on their meals. The food was excellent, the atmosphere even better and the beautiful woman across from him was just the capper.

He'd rarely met a woman who didn't find it necessary to fill every silence with some kind of inane chatter. He found himself relaxing. The silence stretching out between them was companionable somehow, as if they were already a team.

He frowned to himself at that thought, since he hadn't decided a damn thing yet.

"You've lived here your whole life," he said into the quiet.

"Since I was five, yes." She turned her head to look out over the water. The tide was out, and a handful of couples strolled the beach in the moonlight. "It's a lovely island. The town is small, but the hotel is a big draw. Most people prefer coming here because Grandfather's never allowed the cruise ships to stop. So, our guests tend to be very wealthy and very into their privacy. But they spend plenty of money in the village and the shops usually make enough money to last them through the off-season."

"I know." He gave her a quick grin. "The Kings do research, too."

"Then you already know that Tesoro is the perfect spot for the resort you want to build," she said, setting her fork and knife down.

"Agreed." It was more than perfect. Like it had been designed specifically for the plans Rico had in mind. Rico's hotel in Mexico was top-of-the-line, modern, beautiful and plush. But for the resort on Tesoro, things would be different. Rico wanted to go with island elegance. To make this the most talked-about destination spot in the world.

And with King Construction behind the building and

design, it would be. Sean was itching to get started. The plans were already drawn up, the equipment ready to ship to the island. All they needed was the old man's go-ahead and things could start rolling.

"It would be good for Tesoro, too," she told him. "We have a small construction company on the island, you know. My grandfather started it twenty years ago. They do all the building and would be a big help to your company."

"Uh-huh." He knew that, too. Of course the Kings would bring in some of their own men because they'd worked with them for years and trusted them. But using island labor would not only move things along quicker, it would make for good relations with the locals.

It would all be perfect—if he didn't mind getting married to accomplish it.

Melinda's eyes shone in the candlelight and her smile curved her lips just to the point where he thought about leaning over the table to have a taste. Her teeth chewed at her bottom lip again and he felt an answering tug inside him. Sean was tight and hard and going to damn well embarrass himself if he had to stand up anytime soon.

"Are you listening to me?"

"What?" He grinned, grateful for the distraction. "Sure. Construction. Can't get enough of that."

She frowned and huffed out a breath. "I'm just saying that this could be a good deal for all of us, Sean. You get the land, the island gets a hotel that will create jobs and bring in money to the locals—"

"And you get your trust fund."

"Yes." She picked up her wineglass and took the last sip. When she'd finished, she asked, "Well. What do you say? Do we have a deal? Will you marry me?"

Those four words sent an instinctive chill down his

spine, but Sean ignored it. Sure, he had vowed to never again make the mistake of getting married. But this was different.

The first time he had said "I do," he got screwed, in more ways than one. This time, he would get something out of the deal beyond a quickie divorce. This time, he would be the one in charge. The one to say when it was over. The one to walk away.

And this time, his heart wouldn't be involved.

Nodding, he held out one hand to her. "I think you've got a deal."

That smile of hers widened and nearly took his breath away. She took his hand and, just like their first touch hours ago, the instant their palms met, there was a quick flash of heat that seemed to zing straight up his arm to bounce around his chest like a crazed ping-pong ball. Sean had been hoping to hell he had imagined that sizzle between them. But if anything, it was stronger this time around. Damn it. If she felt it, she didn't show it, so neither did Sean. He willed his body into submission and fought against an attraction that was more powerful than he'd expected.

"There's just one more thing," she said as she pulled her hand free of his.

Sean laughed. "You've already swept me off my feet," he said wryly. "What's left?"

"No sex."

Well, *that* got his attention. He stared at her for a long minute until she finally shifted her gaze from his nervously.

This was an entirely new experience for Sean. Most women were downright *eager* to get close to him. Hell, he usually had to fend off women trying to fling themselves into his bed. He'd turned down a lovely woman only an hour ago in the hotel bar. But her blond hair and brown eyes hadn't done a thing for him since he had been too preoccupied with thoughts of Melinda Stanford.

The woman who wanted to marry him—just not sleep with him.

He stared her down and she didn't flinch. That steady blue gaze never wavered.

What was going on? He wasn't imagining the sizzle of heat that leapt between them whenever they touched. He hadn't missed the flash of something interested in her eyes. And he for damn sure wasn't wrong about his own desire for the woman who had turned this trip upside down inside of a few hours. If he'd met her somewhere else, he would have tried to seduce her into a long weekend—and he had no doubt he would have succeeded.

So what was the problem?

"No sex."

"That's right." She took a long breath and looked back into his eyes. "Why complicate things? This is a business arrangement, after all. It's not a *real* marriage, so I don't see why we should..."

"Have sex," he finished for her, astonishment clear in his voice.

"Exactly."

"This just gets better and better," he murmured.

"It's only for two months," she pointed out, managing to sound both impatient and pained all at the same time. "Surely that won't kill you."

"I think I can manage to hang on," he said, though silently he admitted that it wouldn't be a party. He already wanted her and he'd only known her for a few hours. Being married to her, with her all the time...how much worse was this going to get over two months?

Maybe he should just make a call to Rico and find out if

he was willing to put his hotel somewhere else. A moment later, though, he dismissed the idea. It was Tesoro or not at all. The island was perfect for their needs, damn it.

The island had a mystique with people. The hotel was old-school deluxe, but it was small and couldn't support many guests. Since the island was privately held, anyone wanting to do business on Tesoro had to go through Walter Stanford. And he was a man who liked his privacy.

Which would be perfect for the exclusive resort the Kings were planning. The mega-wealthy would come here to play on the beach and enjoy the high life away from throngs of tourists and, most especially, paparazzi.

It was all perfect.

Except for the whole marriage thing.

"And," she said, dragging his attention back to her.

"There's *more*?" he asked with a short laugh. "What else is there? Got a dungeon you want to shut me up in? Or maybe you want me living on bread and water for a couple months?"

"Don't be ridiculous," she said.

"Oh, *I'm* being ridiculous." He shook his head and gave her an almost admiring glance. "You want us to be married. Living together. Putting on a 'colorful truth' for your grandfather—but none of the fun stuff."

She shifted uncomfortably in her chair and he knew for a fact that she was feeling what he was. So just how long would she last with this little celibacy rule? As that thought wandered through his mind, Sean smiled to himself. This, he thought, could get very interesting.

"This isn't about fun—"

"Clearly," he agreed.

Her lips thinned and her mouth worked as if words were trying to get out, but she refused to let them. Finally, though, she took a breath and said patiently, "It's a small island, Sean. So you won't be able to sleep with anyone else, either. My grandfather would find out and this whole thing would be over before it began."

Sean stiffened at the insinuation. Sitting up straight, he laid both hands on the tabletop and leaned in toward her. Even riding that quick whip of anger, he kept his voice down. His gaze bored into hers as he said, "I. Don't. Cheat. When I give my word, I keep it."

Their gazes locked for several long seconds before she finally nodded. "I'm sorry. I just wanted to be clear about everything."

He leaned back in his chair, gritting his teeth against the bubble of frustration inside him. "Fine. We're clear."

"And we still have a deal?"

He looked into those blue eyes of hers again and told himself this was surely a mistake. He felt it right down to his bones. But damned if Sean could see another way for him to get what he wanted.

"Yeah," he said. "We have a deal."

He couldn't believe he was going to do this. Couldn't believe he was going to get married. Again. And this one wouldn't be any more real than the first one.

At least this time though, he'd know going in that the marriage would mean nothing.

Three

Walter Stanford was somewhere in his seventies, but his sharp blue eyes didn't miss much. He was tall, with snowy white hair, a hard jaw and the bearing of a much younger man. He stood behind the wide desk in his library and looked at Sean with a cool, dispassionate eye.

Sean met the older man stare for stare, never blinking. He knew how to run a negotiation and knew all too well that the first man who spoke, lost power. So he kept quiet and waited for the older man to say something.

Walter Stanford's suite took up half of the entire top floor of the hotel, with Melinda's private quarters in the other half. It was old-world elegant, again with just a touch of shabbiness. As if the place had seen better times. Sean had to wonder if the old man was as wealthy as rumor suggested.

He had noticed a couple of telltale water marks on the ceiling, proof of a leaky roof that hadn't been fixed in time. And there were other things too. Nothing over the top, he thought, just tiny warning flags. Scars on the wood floors, chipped molding, window casements where the plaster had crumbled.

Of course, none of that proved anything. All it might mean was that Walter Stanford was simply too busy or too uninterested to make the dozens of minor repairs buildings always required. Or, he thought, it could mean that the old man needed this hotel deal far more than he wanted the Kings to know.

Sean smiled to himself, but kept his expression carefully neutral.

"You've met my granddaughter," Walter said, taking a seat in the bloodred desk chair.

"Yes. She seems...nice," he offered, enjoying using her own word.

The three of them had spent the last twenty minutes chatting and talking about the island. Melinda had left the room just a moment ago and, Sean thought, Walter wasn't wasting any time.

"Let me be frank," the older man said, setting his elbows on the desktop and steepling his fingers. "You want to build a hotel on my island. I want my granddaughter happy."

Sean took a seat in the chair opposite the desk and set one foot atop the other knee and prepared to play dumb. "What's one have to do with the other?"

Walter gave him a smile and a wink. "You're single. Wealthy. Reasonably good-looking."

Wryly, Sean said, "Thank you."

Tucking his fingertips beneath his chin, Walter continued. "I believe in laying my cards out on the table, how about you?"

"Always best to know what the other man's holding."

"Excellent. Then let's get down to business. I want you to marry my granddaughter. Once you've done that, the land is yours."

If Melinda hadn't prepared him for this yesterday, Sean thought, he would have fallen out of his chair. Even prepared, even with a deal already in place, he was a little surprised. Amazing to think that in the twenty-first century, women were still being bartered.

Of course, *this* woman had done the bartering herself and damned if she hadn't negotiated a hell of a deal.

Walter was waiting for an answer and Sean let him wait. His brain raced with the implications of what he was about to agree to. Getting married, even temporarily, was a huge step. He didn't want to, but he had spent the better part of last night lying awake trying to come up with a different way to get what he wanted—and he'd come up empty.

Just as, no doubt, Melinda had known he would.

The Stanfords, both of them, were stubborn enough to be Kings.

Tapping his fingers against his knee, Sean asked, "How does Melinda feel about this?"

Walter frowned briefly. "She understands. It's good for her. Good for the family. Good for the island."

Unexpectedly, a ripple of anger washed through Sean. If Melinda hadn't stepped up to chart her own course and make her own deal with Sean, she would have been no more than a bound sacrifice, stretched out across the Stanford altar.

Good for the island.

Who did things like that now?

Frowning, Sean watched the older man and tried to read his eyes. But the old guy must have been a hell of a poker player back in the day. His expression gave away nothing.

"Well?" The older man dropped both hands to the black blotter on his desk. "What do you say?"

There was a lot he should say, Sean thought. He should tell the old man that his granddaughter was worth more than a bargaining chip to be used in a deal. Hell, a couple of hours spent with her had told Sean that much. He should say that Melinda had a sharp mind and a clever way of driving a bargain. He should tell both of the Stanfords to go to hell and take their island with them.

He'd love to tell him that his granddaughter was filling up his mind with tempting thoughts that were destined to go nowhere. That one touch of her hand was enough to set off fires inside him that were still burning hours later.

But he couldn't tell him that either, so Sean would say nothing about any of it.

"Agreed," he heard himself say and saw the flicker of surprise in the old man's eyes. Apparently, he couldn't disguise everything he was feeling. Or didn't care to.

"Really. That easily?" He leaned back in his chair and the springs creaked. "You'll forgive me, but I'm curious as to your quick acceptance."

Sean smiled. "Changing your mind already?"

"Not at all." Walter spread his hands wide. "I only thought it would take more to convince you."

"Melinda's a beautiful woman," he said, remembering the flash of her blue eyes as she looked at him before leaving the room a few minutes ago.

"She is—but there's more to her than her beauty," her grandfather pointed out.

"I'm sure you're right," Sean agreed, though he already knew firsthand just what a clever mind Melinda had. "Once we're married, we'll have plenty of time to find out all about each other."

"Hmm…"

"I assume you've already checked me out," Sean said. Knowing Melinda had researched him assured Sean that her grandfather had done so as well.

"I have."

Sean nodded. "You made the offer. I accepted. End of story."

Walter was watching him as if waiting for Sean to change his mind. Sean fought another smile. The man had wheeled and dealed his granddaughter to a stranger and now that the stranger had agreed, the old man was having second thoughts? Too late for that. They had a deal and the Kings would soon be arriving to get the project underway.

Pushing up from his chair, Sean stretched out his right hand and said, "I'll just go tell my bride the good news. Then I'll phone my brothers and let them know we can get started on the hotel right away."

Walter stood up too, took Sean's hand and shook it. When he released him again, the older man said, "You can start construction the day after the wedding."

Both of Sean's eyebrows went up. "Don't trust me to go through with it?"

"If I didn't trust you," Walter said softly, "you wouldn't be marrying my granddaughter. Let's just say I prefer to have all of my bases covered."

"Fine," Sean agreed with a nod. "I'll have our lawyers fax you the paperwork this afternoon."

"And *my* lawyer will have a contract for you to sign as well."

Sean's gaze locked with the older man's and for just an instant, there was a silent conversation between them. Two men, each of them powerful, each of them walking into this bargain with their eyes wide open and each of them thinking about the woman at the center of it all.

Hope you know what you're starting here.
You and my granddaughter will work out fine.

If that's what the old guy believed, Sean thought grimly, then he was way off base. And for just an instant, he felt guilty about tricking Walter Stanford. Then he remembered it hadn't been his idea and if Melinda was comfortable with this setup, then why should he mind?

Sean smiled. "I'll go see Melinda and tell her it's settled."

"Fine, fine," Walter told him with a dismissive wave of his hand. "Perhaps you could join me later for a private dinner where we can discuss your plans for the future? Shall we say seven? Here, in my suite?"

Sean eyed the older man. "Sure, I'll see you later, then. Meanwhile, I'm guessing you'll handle all the details of the wedding?"

Walter nodded. "By the end of the week, you'll be a married man."

End of the week.

That rang a gong with the tone of finality inside his head. But Sean ignored it. He'd made his decision, and he wouldn't go back on it now.

"Melinda's a strong woman with a good heart. See that you remember that."

"I will." Sean left the room then, in search of the 'good-hearted' bride who drove a bargain like no one else he had ever known.

The next morning was a disaster.

Sean stared at his computer screen, waiting for his phone call to go through. He caught his own reflection staring back at him and winced. Even in the hazy mirror of the screen, he looked like death. That would teach him to drink brandy with an old man who probably had the stuff flowing through his veins.

But Stanford had wanted to toast their bargain. Since this was supposed to be real, Sean hadn't been able to think of a reason not to. Hours later, after listening to stories of island life and Melinda's childhood, all washed down with glass after glass of expensive brandy, Sean had staggered to his room.

He'd lain awake, waiting for the room to stop spinning before finally falling asleep. Then he'd been chased in his dreams by a wildly laughing Stanford waving a giant brandy bottle at him while Melinda threw bouquet after bouquet at his head.

"Don't even want that dream analyzed," he murmured.

All he really wanted at the moment was to quiet the jackhammers behind his eyes. He coughed and his head almost exploded. Moaning softly, he was reaching for a bottle of aspirin when his brother Rafe's face came up on the screen.

"Sean—" He paused and frowned. "Damn. You look like hell."

Thanks to videophone conferencing, there was no disguising his hangover. For the first time in his life, Sean cursed technology. "Yeah, thanks Rafe. Nice to see you, too."

His brother's eyes narrowed thoughtfully. "Are you hungover?"

"Brilliant observation," Sean said tightly as he struggled with the cap on the aspirin bottle. Childproof, okay. But did they have to seal the damn thing as if it contained the nuclear codes for Armageddon?

"Hard to miss, what with the dark circles under your eyes and the way you're cringing in the sunlight like a vampire away from his crypt."

God, why hadn't he waited to call until later? Or at least closed the drapes? Well, he knew why he hadn't done that. It had just seemed too taxing at the time.

"What's going on?" Rafe asked. "Did you get the deal?"

"The deal. About that…"

"Damn it, Sean," Rafe shouted.

"Can you dial it down a notch or two?" Sean rubbed at the spot between his eyes even though he knew it wouldn't do any good. He finally managed to get the aspirin bottle open and tapped two tablets onto his palm. Then he tapped out two more. Desperate times.

He washed them all down with a long gulp of water from the bottle on his desk and prayed they were miracle aspirins, about to kick in and restore him to health in the next thirty seconds.

No luck.

Rafe grumbled, took a breath and said, "Fine. I'm calm. Now tell me what's going on?"

"It's a long story," Sean said, rubbing his eyes. "And I'd rather tell it only once. Is Lucas in the office?"

"That doesn't sound good," Rafe muttered, "but yeah. He's here." Reaching to one side of his desk, he hit a button and said, "Marie, get Lucas in here, will you? Thanks."

"Marie? New assistant?" Sean asked.

"Yeah," Rafe admitted. "Katie insisted I hire somebody to help me so I can get home in time for dinner every night."

His brother might sound like he was complaining, but Sean knew how nuts about his wife Rafe really was. And who could blame him? Rafe could be a pain in the ass at times, but his wife was a peach. Not to mention, she made the best cookies in the known universe.

"How's Katie?" Sean managed to ask.

"She's great," Rafe said and a soft smile curved his

mouth. Amazing the changes Katie had made to the formerly surly Rafe King. "She says I should tell you she's saving a batch of her pistachio chocolate mint cookies for you."

Sean swallowed hard. Ordinarily, that would have been a nice surprise. At the moment though, it felt like live snakes were writhing in his belly. Still, it was the thought that counted. "Tell her thanks."

Rafe frowned at Sean's less than enthusiastic reply, then waved Lucas over when he came into the room. In a second or two, Lucas was sitting beside Rafe so that both of them could be seen.

"Damn," Lucas said, pulling his head back in shock. "You look like hell."

Sean sighed. "That's the consensus. How's the baby?"

"Danny's great," Lucas said, grinning. "I swear he said Daddy this morning."

Sean laughed and was rewarded with another jolt of pain. Since his new nephew was barely three months old, that wasn't likely. But Lucas was convinced his son was a genius. And who was Sean to argue?

"On topic, guys? Are you out there partying with some blonde when you should be doing business?" Rafe asked.

"Because the blondes can wait until we get the damn land," Lucas put in.

"He doesn't need to be dating *any* blondes when he's there to work," Rafe argued.

"I agree, but he's not dead and he's not married, Rafe. God, I thought Katie had lightened you up a little."

"I don't *need* lightening up."

His brothers' voices were getting louder and the pain in Sean's head just kept growing. He tried to tune out the argument taking place back in Long Beach, California. But Kings were hard to ignore. Even for one of the family.

Rafe and Lucas could go on for hours and Sean knew it. Their argument would slide from Sean to their current project and might even drift to old grudges from when they were all kids.

He smiled in spite of his headache. *All* of his brothers were close. Their father, Ben King, had never married any of the women who bore his many sons, but every summer, he gathered his sons together at his ranch in California. For three months every year, the King boys were real brothers and they had forged a bond that had only gotten stronger over the years.

Sean's smile faded a bit as he thought about his parents. Ben had done the best he could, he knew. But Sean's mother had been too fragile to deal with life. Too…breakable to leave the man she had eventually married, even when the abuse began and—

"Sean!"

He came up out of the misery of his memories with a grateful start. Looking at his brothers' identical expressions, he cleared his throat and said, "There is no blonde."

"Well that's something anyway," Rafe muttered.

"She's got black hair," Sean said. But that didn't describe Melinda's hair either. More like the color of deepest night, when a man's dreams and fantasies came to life. When a woman with eyes like hers and a touch that was all heat could turn even the strongest man into Jell-O.

He sighed, letting her memory fill his mind and reverberate throughout his body. This was going to be a *long* couple of months, he told himself. Not being able to touch her was going to take every ounce of self-control he possessed. Because he had known her for about twenty-four hours and *already* wanted her. Bad.

"I knew there'd be a woman," Lucas said, almost

proudly. But then, Sean thought, maybe his brother was living vicariously now that he was married.

"Let him talk." The voice of reason from Rafe. Amazing, Sean thought. Katie really was a miracle worker.

"I thought we were meeting about the hotel project," Lucas grumbled. "I'm not interested in hearing about Sean's latest conquest."

That was all it took for the two of them to run away with the conversation again. If he were back home, in the office, Sean would be munching on cookies and using his smartphone to check in on customer bases and suppliers. Here, he was lucky just to be sitting upright.

Sunlight was bright in the hotel room, but thankfully, the desk where he was sitting was positioned so that his back was to the bay window. He knew that out the window lay a fantastic view of the harbor and pristine aqua-blue ocean, if he was interested—which he wasn't at the moment. It was way too bright out there.

His hotel room at the Stanford hotel was the kind of plush he could only guess would have been considered five stars fifty years ago. Their one big concession to modern life seemed to be the high-speed internet service and the minibars. Otherwise, he might have been on an old movie set.

There were no flat-screen TVs or high-end bathrooms or, hell, even hairdryers or in-room coffee setups. And yet, there was something quietly…elegant here that no modern hotel could ever hope to claim.

"Okay, fine," Lucas was telling Rafe. "I'll listen to Sean if you'll keep quiet."

Sean laughed, then winced as his headache pounded.

"What's this about Sean?" Rafe asked in a quiet, even tone that had Sean silently thanking him.

"I don't even know where to begin," he admitted. It had

been a wild twenty-four hours and he wasn't sure even he completely believed what had happened.

"Start with the land," Lucas prodded. "Do we have the deal or not?"

Sean pulled in a deep breath, then took another long gulp of water while his brothers waited impatiently.

"Well?" Rafe asked.

Snorting a choked-off laugh, Sean said, "There's some good news and some bad news."

"Perfect," Rafe muttered.

"Start with the good," Lucas told him. "It'll give me strength for the rest of it.

"Okay, good news is, we got the deal."

Rafe and Lucas both laughed in relief. "Well, why the hell didn't you say so?" Rafe crowed.

"I knew you could do it," Lucas said. "I told Rose just last night that nobody can stand against Sean when he turns on the King charm."

"Hmm…" He would have agreed a couple of days ago. But, since meeting Melinda Stanford, he had to admit that his charm apparently had limits. She hadn't proposed to him because she was blown away by his wit and seductive powers. And she sure as hell wasn't tumbling into his bed. Yet.

"Okay," Rafe said. "Let's have the bad news."

"How bad can it be?" Lucas said, still grinning. "We got the deal. We can start construction right away and—"

"Let him finish," Rafe said without taking his gaze from Sean's.

Sean kept his eyes fixed on Rafe, since there was no point in trying to avoid it anyway. "Okay, the thing is, looks like I'm getting married."

Silence.

His brothers just stared at him. Then they turned to look

at each other before shifting their gazes back to Sean in a move that was so smooth it looked choreographed.

"Married?" Rafe said.

"Are you nuts?" Lucas asked.

"The black-haired woman?" Rafe asked.

"The very one," Sean told them. "Melinda Stanford."

"Walter's granddaughter. That's why the phone call."

Sean looked at Lucas and nodded.

"You met her, fell in love and proposed all in twenty-four hours?" Rafe demanded, his voice hitching higher with every word.

Sean stiffened. "Who said anything about love?"

"Then what the hell, Sean?"

"I made a deal with Melinda. We get married, the Kings get the land."

"Oh hell no," Rafe argued. Clearly outraged, his spine went stiff and his chin jutted out as if he were stepping into a knock-down, drag-out fight.

"This is 'taking one for the team' to a whole new level," Lucas put in.

Sean rubbed one hand across his face and prayed again that the aspirin he took would start working before his head exploded. "It's done. I made the deal, and I'll stick with it."

"Why would you do that?"

He snapped, "I didn't see any other way to get the property."

"You're out of your mind."

"No, I'm not," Sean said, reeling in the irritation starting to churn inside. "It's a temporary thing. Two months and we'll get a divorce. But the Kings will still have the land."

Lucas shook his head as if he couldn't think of anything to say—which under other circumstances might have been funny. Rafe, on the other hand, wasn't having that problem.

"You can't do this, Sean," he said tightly. "Getting married knowing you're getting a divorce just isn't—"

"What," he asked, "*right*?"

"What I want for you," his older brother finished pointedly. "When you get married it should damn well mean something."

Sean gritted his teeth and bit back the words he wanted to say. That getting married didn't mean anything to some people. That he'd already tried marriage a long time ago and wasn't interested in repeating that mistake. That the only reason he had agreed to this farce was so that his family could get what they needed—and because he had an escape clause written into the bargain.

His brothers were happily married to wonderful women they each loved desperately. They would never understand Sean's point of view. And why would they? His brothers didn't know that Sean had already been married once before. In fact, no one knew about that very brief, very *messy* marriage and divorce and that was how he wanted it.

Kings made mistakes, sure. But they didn't talk about them and they for damn sure didn't share their feelings about them. It had been Sean's mistake, and he'd cleaned it up. Dredging it back up now wouldn't serve any purpose at all.

When he felt like he could speak without clenching his teeth even tighter, Sean said, "Don't think of it as a marriage. Just a merger."

"Damn strange way to do business," Lucas muttered.

"Strange or not, we're getting what we want out of it," Sean told them. And that's what he had to keep uppermost in his mind. This was for the Kings. For their future.

Going into business on this hotel with their cousin Rico would take their construction company to an even higher level than where they already were and that was something that was worth any risk. "Walter's going to have the deed to the property drawn up for our signatures before the wedding."

"Which is when?" Rafe wanted to know.

"By the end of the week," Sean said and swallowed hard as if there were a noose around his neck, tightening. Ridiculous. He had agreed to this, and he wouldn't back out.

"A week?" Lucas stared at him, stunned.

"Tell us when," Rafe said. "We'll be there."

"No." Sean shook his head, in spite of the throbbing behind his eyes.

"What do you mean, no?" Lucas demanded, with a glance at Rafe to make sure he was just as pissed.

He was.

"Of course we'll be there for you, you moron," Rafe said. "We're not going to let you do this on your own."

"Damn it, Rafe," Sean said, "it's not like this is the real deal. It's business and that's all it is."

"Doesn't seem right not being there," Lucas muttered. "We support each other. Always have. Always will."

He smiled in spite of everything, grateful for his brothers and the strong family ties they had. But love his brothers or not, he didn't want them there for the wedding. There was just no point. And damned if he'd listen to Rafe and Lucas—or worse yet, Katie and Rose—giving him grief for doing what he knew he had to do.

"It's fine," Sean insisted, meaning every word. "It'll be easier on me if you're not here."

"Won't Stanford expect your family to be there?"

Damn. Wincing, he silently acknowledged that he hadn't really considered that.

"Probably," he admitted, but shook his head again anyway. "I'll just tell him it happened too fast for you guys to get out here."

"Yeah, that'll go over big," Rafe muttered.

"Look," Sean told them both with a tired sigh, "I'll take care of the details here. You guys get hold of Rico and tell him we're on. I'll check out the small construction company here on the island, see what we can use and what we'll need to bring in."

"I've got a cargo ship putting out to sea in a week or so," Rafe said. "We can get most of our equipment onboard and get to work as soon as possible."

"Sounds good," Sean said, relieved to be back on safer terrain. Talking about the job, the business, he felt more in control. "With the weather here, it being fall won't be a problem. We should be able to keep the job running right through winter without many weather delays."

"Sounds good," Lucas told him with a grin. "Rico's going to want to jump into this project. Oh, and he's having us build him a house on the island too. Guess he's decided to make Tesoro his main residence."

Sean held up one hand. "All I negotiated for was the hotel property. Rico's on his own with the house deal."

"Seriously," Lucas muttered with a snort, "what do you have left to bargain with? Your *soul*?"

"Funny," Sean told him.

"Oh, Rico's got the land for the house," Rafe told him. "Walter had no problem with that. It was the beachfront property he was hanging onto. Until now."

"Yeah," Sean said, feeling that metaphorical noose tightening around his throat again. "Until now."

"Are you sure you're okay with this?" Rafe asked.

"Why wouldn't I be?" Sean answered his question with a question and let it go.

"Always were the most stubborn one of us," Lucas said.

"Yeah, right." Rafe laughed. "You make *Dad* look reasonable."

"No reason to be insulting," Lucas countered.

"You want insulting?" Rafe argued.

Sean smiled to himself as he watched his brothers fall into a familiar argument. They were in California, but they might as well have been on Mars for as far away as Sean felt from the family he loved. But it was better this way, he told himself.

No reason for them to meet Melinda or to celebrate a marriage that had a two-month expiration date.

He'd made the deal and he'd stick to it. But damned if he'd have an audience for it.

Four

"You're doing *what*?"

"I'm getting married," Melinda said and waited for the crushing, debilitating panic she kept expecting to set in. It didn't, which was completely weird because if anyone had the right to panic, it was her.

After Sean and her grandfather had had their meeting, she'd spent five quick minutes with the man who would soon be her husband. Sean hadn't said much, just told her that it was set and that he was going to have dinner with her grandfather. Then he told her he'd call her sometime today. Which, so far, he hadn't.

She shot a quick look out the kitchen window. It was only late morning. Still plenty of time. So why was her stomach doing a jittery dance and her throat occasionally closing up so even breathing was becoming an Olympic event?

Oh, God.

She had spent all of last night, sitting on the terrace of her hotel suite, staring out at the ocean. The trade winds ruffled through the leaves of the trees and the scent of night-blooming jasmine had wrapped itself around her and still, she couldn't find any peace.

And she knew why.

Sean King was too attractive. Too...*something*. He got to her in a way no man had since Steven and just admitting that should have been enough to have her backing out of the deal she had struck. But she couldn't do that. Not and win her independence.

So here she sat, at her best friend's kitchen table, trying to convince herself that everything would be okay. Only problem being, now that the deed was done, everything was in motion and Melinda was beginning to feel like she was strapped into a runaway roller coaster. Her grandfather was happy. Sean was...she wasn't sure how he was feeling. And she was, anxious. But resolved.

"I can't believe this." Kathy Clark, Melinda's best friend and absolutely the only person she could talk to about this, shook her head. "You're the one who said what your grandfather was trying to do was medieval."

"I know, but—"

"And you swore that if he ever tried to marry you off again you'd join a convent."

"Yes, but—"

"*And*, you said that you couldn't marry anyone because you're still in love with...Steven."

Melinda heard the hesitation in her friend's voice and frowned. Kathy never had liked Steven and Melinda was never sure why. But that wasn't the point now anyway.

Kathy frowned at her as she held a baby bottle to her son's mouth. "So who is this mystery man and why did you agree to something you practically took a blood oath to avoid?"

When she paused for breath, Melinda jumped into the conversation. "This is different. My grandfather didn't arrange this, *I* did."

Her friend blinked big brown eyes and shook her head harder. "Okay, that actually makes *negative* sense."

Melinda laughed and reached down to pick up Kathy's two-year-old daughter. Setting the tiny girl onto her lap, she brushed baby-fine hair off the child's forehead and said, "It makes perfect sense, Kath. I'm going to marry Sean and get my trust fund and then we'll get a quiet divorce."

"Just like that."

"Yep." Melinda planted a kiss on top of Danielle's head and smiled when the little girl slapped both hands together.

"Uh-huh."

She looked up at the tone in Kathy's voice and found her friend watching her through narrowed eyes. "What?"

"Getting married, even temporarily, is a huge step. And sometimes divorces, even the ones you want, are more painful than you might think. Are you really sure you want to do this?"

"Of course I'm sure," she argued, keeping her voice light and singsongy to please the toddler on her lap. "There won't be any pain in this divorce and there won't be any hard feelings, either. We both get what we want. Me, my trust fund, and my new husband will get the land he wants. I've thought it all out, covered every possibility and this really is the answer."

"It's a weird world when you consider marrying a complete stranger a good thing."

"He's not a stranger. I researched him."

"Oh. Well then. My mistake," Kathy told her and set the

baby bottle aside when her son finished his lunch. Lifting the six-month-old to her shoulder she patted his back while looking at Melinda. "Instead of your grandfather selling you, you put yourself on the open market."

"And got a better price," Melinda told her, grinning when her friend sighed. "Look, it's going to be great. I'll get married, get my trust fund and then I'll be single again and life will go on."

"Uh-huh."

"Sean has already agreed to it, even the part where I told him I wouldn't be sleeping with him."

"This just gets better and better," Kathy murmured.

"Funny, that's just what Sean said." Melinda straightened the tiny yellow bow on the baby's curls.

"Sean who? Who is this lucky groom?"

"Hmm?" Melinda smiled down at Danielle, then looked at Kathy. "Sean King."

Kathy's jaw dropped. "Sean *King*? *The* Sean King? The guy in all the magazines? The one with mega millions? The one with the black hair and blue eyes and great ass?"

Melinda put both hands over Danielle's ears. Laughing, she said, "Kathy!"

"I don't believe this." She set her infant son into the bouncy seat beside them on the kitchen table. Instantly, Cameron started kicking, sending the little mobile of birds over his head into blind flight.

Kathy stood up and went for more coffee. She filled both of their cups, then set the coffeepot back down onto the stove. When she took her seat again, she looked at Melinda and said, "You know I love you, but you are asking for trouble with this, honey."

"Kath, it's gonna be fine." Though looking into her friend's worried eyes sent the tiniest spirals of anxiety unwinding through Melinda's system.

It was natural that Kathy would react like this. She and her husband Tom loved each other like crazy. So of course she would look at a marriage of convenience like it was a prison sentence.

"Sean King could have any woman in the known universe," Kathy told her. "Heck, we live on an island in the middle of nowhere and *we* know who he is!"

"Well yes, but—"

"He's rich and gorgeous and probably arrogant, most men like him are...."

"Because you've known so many men like Sean King," Melinda stated.

"I don't have to know them to know them, you know?"

Melinda blinked. "Sadly, I understood that."

Picking up her coffee cup, Kathy took a sip, then cradled the mug between her hands. "I'm just saying that you could be setting yourself up for something you're not prepared for."

Danielle squirmed on Melinda's lap, so she set the little girl down and watched her toddle off to her play stove on the other side of the room.

Melinda and Kathy had been friends for fifteen years. Ever since Kathy's family had moved to the island when her father took over the job as manager of the hotel. When Kathy married a man born and raised on Tesoro, Melinda had stood up for her, and she was godmother to both of their children.

Kathy's house was always a chaos-filled sanctuary for Melinda. So different from the quiet elegance of the hotel and the owner's penthouse suites where she had grown up and still lives, this cottage always felt warm and welcoming. As if it were alive with the love that saturated its walls.

There was a time when Melinda had dreamed about

having a place like this—a *life* like this. With a husband who loved her and children to hold. But that dream died with Steven more than a year ago now and Melinda had buried it along with her fiancé. Now, what she wanted was her independence. A chance to live her life the way she wanted to, without the loving interference of a concerned grandfather.

"I know what I'm doing, really."

Kathy met her stare and sighed. "I hope so." Then shrugging, she asked, "So, when's the wedding?"

Melinda grinned. "Next Saturday, and you're the matron of honor."

"Next Saturday?" Kathy's jaw dropped and her eyes took on a horrified sheen. "I can't lose ten pounds in a week!"

Still smiling, Melinda listened as her friend talked about manicures, shopping for dresses and who she could get to watch the kids for the day.

Worried or not, Kathy would be there for her, Melinda knew that. But as her friend's warnings repeated over and over again in her mind, Melinda had to wonder if she was as sure about all of this as she was pretending to be.

The next few days passed in a blink.

Or at least it seemed that way to Sean. He didn't see much of Melinda, but then why should he? This was nothing more than a business deal—though dressed up a lot prettier than most. And to keep his mind off the fact that he was about to get *married*, Sean spent his time exploring a bit of the island.

He had already spent a day or two with the Stanford construction team. It was a small outfit—but they knew the island and how to build. Sean was impressed with them and knew Rafe and Lucas would be, too. Having knowledgeable, on-the-spot workers around when the project got going would come in handy. Plus, using local guys would go a long way toward making the King invasion a welcome one.

On his own, he'd driven the circumference of the island, noting the differences in the land as he went. Some areas of Tesoro were practically barren while most of the island boasted forests and flowers and waterfalls. There was no airstrip on the island and Sean knew his brothers would want to build something for private planes. He'd spotted a clearing near the hotel that would do if they could talk Walter into it. Otherwise, as it stood now, the only way to reach the island was to fly into St. Thomas then take a boat to Tesoro. Granted, they were fast boats, but if the Kings could set up a private airstrip, that would make things even easier on the wealthy guests they planned on enticing to the hotel.

For now though, Sean was exploring the village, where shops stood ready to welcome the tourists who made up their economy. Tesoro was one of the bigger privately held islands. About three thousand acres, with beautiful beaches, forests and more flowers than Sean could remember seeing anywhere.

The village was so picturesque it was like taking a walk through a postcard. Every shop was neatly tended and each of them was painted a different, pastel color—blue, pink, yellow and green.

Brightly colored flowers tumbled out of terra-cotta pots lining the sidewalk. The view from above would be like staring down at a fallen rainbow. Windows glistened in the sun and doors stood open in welcome.

For a man used to living in crowded Southern California, this was like being in Brigadoon.

He smiled to himself at the thought. He wouldn't

even have had that reference if not for Lucas's wife. She had been watching the old movie one Saturday when he stopped in to beg a meal. In exchange, Rose had forced him to watch the damn thing with her.

So, that magical village in Scotland, where everything was beautiful and everyone was happy seemed a pretty appropriate comparison.

He could see why Walter protected this island so staunchly. Sean paused to look around, letting his gaze take in the people, the flowers, the quiet sense of tranquility—and then tried to imagine the village swarming with cruise ship tourists. He shuddered just thinking about the influx of loud voices and clacking cameras.

No, it was better this way, he thought, enjoying the otherworldly quiet and the soft, cool breeze that eased the heat of the sun. Unlike most of the Caribbean islands, the trade winds blew almost constantly across Tesoro, keeping not only the heat—but the flying insects at bay. Which, Sean told himself with a smile, would make their future guests happy.

He wandered along the village street, peering in shop windows, taking pictures with his smartphone and sending them via text messaging to his brothers as he went. Rafe and Lucas had both been here, of course, when they tried to make a deal with Walter. But those meetings had been over so quickly, they hadn't been on Tesoro long enough to really look around. It was Rico who had stayed on the island several years ago and ever since had been planning his return.

For the longest time, Sean hadn't understood Rico's fascination with this place. But the more time he spent there, the more Sean got it. There was just something about Tesoro that seemed to reach inside a man and untwist the knots he carried around within. Knots he hadn't even been aware of until they dissipated.

He shook his head at his own rambling thoughts and put it down to pre-wedding nerves. Because God knew, he had a lot more to be anxious about than most would-be grooms. After all, he wasn't getting married for the usual reasons. No more than he had before. Been there, done that, didn't even get the T-shirt, he thought wryly.

A couple of laughing kids charged past him on the sidewalk, and Sean jolted, then laughed at his own idiocy. If he didn't pay attention to what was going on around him, he could end up walking right off a cliff.

The distant, muffled roar of a boat's engine didn't stand a chance against the shouts of a shopkeeper, yelling at the kids to go home. Sean smiled again. Even postcards come to life had a few problems, he supposed, which only made this place more real.

When he spotted the jewelry store, he paused, caught by the display of rings, necklaces and bracelets in the window. There were diamonds and rubies and other gemstones, naturally. But there were also pieces with the blue-green stone Sean had seen Melinda wearing the night they'd had dinner and sealed their bargain.

"Well," he mused aloud, "can't get married without a ring."

Fake marriage or not, it had to at least look real. He stepped through the open door and walked slowly inside, his boot heels hitting the gleaming wood floor like taps from a hammer. It wasn't a big shop, but the display cases were filled with dazzling jewels. He was struck by the flash of color that surrounded him, all of it artfully arranged to show the pieces at their best.

But Sean paid no attention to the ordinary offerings,

instead walking directly to a case where the blue-green stones glittered behind a sheen of glass.

An older man with gray hair and a permanent squint—probably from staring into jewelry loupes for too many years—stepped up with a smile. "You must be Sean King."

Sean started. "Word travels fast."

The man gave an eloquent shrug. "It's a small island and the fact that you and Melinda Stanford are getting married is big news."

"Yeah, I guess it would be." No paparazzi on the island, but apparently the gossips were hard at work anyway. Couldn't really blame people for talking though. Everyone here knew Melinda. Knew the Stanfords. Of course they would be interested in a surprise wedding.

Offering his right hand, he said, "Nice to meet you."

"And you, Mr. King. I'm James Noble, and this is my shop."

"You have some pretty things," Sean told him and watched as pleasure lit the older man's eyes. "And since you know about the wedding, you'll know I'm going to need a ring."

An even wider smile greeted that statement. "Of course. What can I show you?"

"Well," Sean said, going into a squat in front of the display case. "I really like these blue-green stones. They're... different."

And he already knew they looked great on Melinda. But then, he admitted silently, what *wouldn't* look good on her? She was beautiful and as coolly elegant as the old hotel where she lived. She walked, and he was captivated by the sway of her hips. She smiled, and he thought about kissing her. She was...taking up way too many of his thoughts, Sean thought with a frown.

"They certainly are," James told him. "The Tesoro

Topaz is found only on this island, and we are the only shop to carry it."

"Tesoro Topaz?" Sean asked, straightening up as James lifted a white velvet tray out of the case and laid it atop the glass counter.

As Sean took a closer look, the man talked. "The stone is mined here, on the island. Apparently formed millennia ago by volcanic activity. As to why the stone is found only here, I believe it has something to do with the chemical makeup of our lovely island and how it reacted to those now long-dead volcanoes."

Sean looked up at the man and smiled. "Sounds like you've given that speech before."

The man relaxed a bit and returned the smile. "Often," he agreed. "But honestly, most people only care about the stone itself, not how it was formed."

"The stone is pretty, but the craftsmanship of this ring is amazing," Sean said, picking up a ring that had several of the topazes set into a gold band that was etched and detailed so beautifully, it almost looked like lace.

"Ah, yes." James nodded. "The artist is local, and her work is truly breathtaking. Her designs are always in demand."

"I can see why," Sean told him, and took a closer look at the ring. It was small, but then Melinda's fingers were long and narrow. It would probably fit and if it didn't, she could bring it back in here and the artist could size it for her. "I'll take this one."

James gave him a smile and nodded. "I think Melinda will be pleased with your choice."

"Hope so," Sean told him.

"I'll just give it a final polish and box it for you." He was still smiling, but Sean dismissed that as a shopkeeper's pleasure in making a sale.

"That'd be great, thanks." Sean pulled out his wallet and handed over his credit card. "I've got to say I'm a little surprised at the price though. Not that I'm complaining, but you could probably get a lot more for that kind of craftsmanship."

James shrugged again and took out a polishing cloth. "We're a small island with a limited supply of customers."

Sean leaned both hands on the glass case and watched the man's reaction as he asked, "How would you like it if there were more tourists coming to the island?"

"I know about the hotel you're planning to build, if that's what you're asking," James said with a wink.

Sean grinned. "Island gossip chain?"

"Absolutely," the man told him. "You'll find that nothing stays a secret for long on Tesoro."

"Okay," Sean said with a nod. "So, how do you feel about it?"

"Cautiously optimistic," the man said. "I've always agreed with Walter on his no cruise ship stance." He shuddered a little as he said, "I don't like the idea of Tesoro being overrun with thousands of people. But a luxury resort is something different, isn't it?"

"Yeah, it is. Fewer people," Sean said. "Fewer disruptions and a lighter impact on the environment."

"It will still be change," James told him, tucking the ring into a cream-colored velvet box and snapping the lid closed, "but not all change is bad."

"I think you'll be pleased," Sean told him.

"I hope so," James said and rang up the sale. When he was finished, he gave Sean his receipt and said with a grin, "I hope Melinda likes the ring."

"Thanks." Sean's fist closed over the small box. "I'm sure I'll be seeing you around."

"Absolutely. I'll be at the wedding."

Chuckling, Sean nodded and headed for the door. "Along with everyone else on the island?"

"Exactly."

Sean stepped outside, still smiling ruefully. Of course every resident of Tesoro would be at the wedding. The place was so small, they probably all thought of each other as family. The island was a world away from his everyday life. In California, there were so many people, so much... *noise*, a man could hardly hear himself think. He had always liked that—or at least, he had been comfortable with it. Where he lived, in Sunset Beach, he didn't know his neighbors more than to exchange a nod with them in passing. His brothers were his best friends, and the women he spent time with came and went practically unnoticed.

Once, he had wanted more. The kind of "connections" most people searched for. But he'd learned his lesson in a hurry and had backed off immediately after that fiasco, wrapping himself in layers of insulation—using wit and charm to keep deeper emotions at bay.

Now, he was on an island where there was no escaping the kind of closeness he didn't feel comfortable with—and he was about to marry into it.

The ring in his pocket felt heavy enough to be an anchor. Or a ball and chain, he thought grimly. Images of Melinda rose up in his mind again as easily as if they had been etched there permanently. He couldn't escape thoughts of her. Couldn't escape the growl of hunger his body felt. Her eyes, her smile, her quiet determination to have things go her way.

He smiled faintly at that thought. If there was one thing a King could understand—especially, he told himself, *this* King, it was determination. Wanting to win. That didn't mean the next two months were going to be easy though. He knew already that he wanted her. Pretending to have a wife and not being able to touch her was going to make him nuts.

He pulled in a deep breath of the ocean air and told himself it didn't matter. He'd survive. Kings *always* survived.

A couple of months from now, he'd be a free man again.

And Melinda Stanford, beauty, brains and incredible sensuality notwithstanding, would be nothing more than a memory.

Five

The crowd applauded.

Melinda hardly heard them. Instead, she stared up into the eyes of her *husband* and saw a reluctant humor there, shining down at her.

Something inside her warmed and raced through her veins. His hand holding hers, his right arm wrapped around her waist, he held her close enough that Melinda could feel the steady beat of his heart.

Music soared out around them, an old Ella Fitzgerald tune and that smoky, sexy voice seemed to swell in the air. Melinda's eyes filled with a sudden rush of tears. She could hardly believe it was done. She was married.

"Brides don't cry," Sean whispered.

"I know," she said, blinking her tears back determinedly. "It's just…"

"Weird?" he offered, steering her into a tight turn with practiced ease.

"Well, yes." Her gaze fixed on him, she caught snatches of the crowd in her peripheral vision, but they were hardly more than a blur of color.

"I hear that," he said, smiling down at her. "But your grandfather looks happy."

She turned her head slightly to catch a glimpse of Walter, standing on the sidelines, beaming at the dancing couple.

"He does, doesn't he?" A narrow thread of guilt snaked its way through her. She'd made him happy by lying to him. And in the next instant, she imagined his face two months from now when she had to tell him she was getting a divorce. The image wasn't a pleasant one and she closed her eyes in an effort to shut it out.

"Regrets already?" Sean asked.

She considered lying to him, too, but what would be the point? "A few," she admitted. "You?"

"A few," he agreed with a nod. Then his arm around her waist tightened further, pressing her even closer.

It wasn't only the beat of his heart she could feel now, Melinda realized. As he held her tightly to him, she felt the unmistakably hard proof of what he was feeling. Her gaze swept up to meet his again.

He shrugged and gave her a tight smile. "My regrets are a little more personal."

No sex.

Her own body sizzled a bit as he pulled her tightly enough to him that she felt the heavy length of his arousal pushing at her. Melinda's response was instant and instinctive. Damp heat centered at her core and a pulsing ache settled deep inside her. If he noticed her reaction, he didn't let it show, merely continuing their dance smoothly.

While the song played on, Melinda's mind went back over the brief ceremony on the patio of the Stanford hotel.

She had walked down a short, flower-strewn aisle on the arm of her beaming grandfather, and her gaze had locked on Sean. He wore a gray suit, with a crisp white shirt and a dark red tie. His gaze had heated as he watched her approach and she had felt just a small thrill of pleasure at the look in his eyes.

What woman wouldn't have, she'd asked herself? Sean King was all male and seeing raw appreciation in his gaze had started a slow burn inside her that was still smoldering. He was gorgeous, her new husband. And the way he held her now almost made her want to rethink that no-sex pledge she had pushed him into.

But the moment that thought appeared, she banished it. In her mind, she replaced Sean's image with that of Steven, the man who should have been her husband. The man she had loved until the day he died in a tragic car accident. This day should have been about love. Not business. Not a merger.

"You're frowning," Sean told her, dipping his head closer to hers. "Our guests will wonder what I said to upset you."

"What?" She looked up into his lake-blue eyes and fought past the tumult going on inside her.

The song seemed to go and on. Or, she wondered, were these feelings and this hushed conversation really taking no time at all?

"Smile, Melinda. We're married. You won. You've got everything you wanted."

"Not everything," she said softly as the song swelled even higher around them.

"So what's missing?"

His palm splayed against her back and heat from his body slid into hers, fanning those low flames inside her. Flames from a fire that she hadn't expected. Or wanted.

"Nothing," she said quietly, unwilling to bring up Steven to the man she had just married. "It's nothing."

"Okay...so then smile a little or people will wonder why you married me."

She chuckled as she knew he'd meant her to and the moment passed. She looked at the ring on her left hand and wiggled her ring finger to make the light sparkle off the gemstones. "I love my ring," she said.

"I'm glad." He nodded and added, "I saw it in a jewelry shop in town. It's the same stone as the earrings I saw you wearing."

"Tesoro Topaz," she said with a smile.

"Yeah." He turned her again, holding her close as Ella's voice soared. "I thought it was appropriate."

"It's perfect," Melinda assured him with a smile.

"Good. That's good." The music faded away and ended with a sigh as Sean turned her into one last, fast spin that left her breathless. Melinda was caught by his eyes as he stared down at her. She felt her own heartbeat speeding out of control as he gave her a slow smile that curved one corner of his mouth into a flirtatious grin.

The crowd applauded again, but neither of them acknowledged the thunderous noise. Instead they were caught on the empty dance floor, gazes locked.

Intimate strangers.

"A kiss!" Someone in the crowd shouted.

An instant later, that cry was repeated over and over again until it was a chant that filled the ballroom of the Stanford hotel, ringing off the punched tin ceiling and bouncing off the paneled walls.

"We don't have to," Melinda said, her voice swallowed by the noisy urging of their guests.

"Of course we do," Sean said, that smile never wavering. "You want this to look real, right?"

"Yes...but we already kissed at the end of the ceremony."

"That was a dignified peck, not a *kiss*," he said and bent his head to hers. "If we want this to look good then we've got to make this one count—"

Melinda closed her eyes as her new husband swept her into a romantic dip, then covered her mouth with his. A wash of heat, delicious, soul-searing fire, enveloped her in an instant. She hadn't expected *this*. It was just a kiss. And yet, it was so much more.

He took her thoroughly, and Melinda was only vaguely aware of the watching crowd cheering. How could she pay attention to anything else when every square inch of her body was electrified? His tongue tangled with hers and she arched into him, letting him—no—*helping* him to devour her.

It didn't seem to matter that she wasn't in love. Didn't matter that she had never planned on kissing her new husband. All that *did* matter was what he was doing to her. The sensations crashing through her body, her mind.

She'd never known anything like this before. His arms tightened around her until she could hardly draw a breath and she didn't care. She was much too busy trying to make sense of this. How could it happen? How could she feel these sensations blasting through her when she hardly knew him? When he wasn't *Steven*?

That name reverberating in her mind was enough to douse the flames within. She broke the kiss, tearing her head back to stare up at him through astonished eyes. It was small comfort to see the same shock in his eyes she knew was written in her own.

"Now *that* was a wedding kiss!" Her grandfather's voice bellowed out over the others.

In response, Sean eased her up onto her feet. He looked

away from her, but with one smooth move wrapped one arm around her shoulders and tucked her into his side.

His stance was casual, his smile easy, but Melinda felt the rapid thud of his heartbeat and knew he had experienced everything she had during that kiss. Which meant... what?

He had already agreed to the no-sex clause in their bargain. Would he think that one amazing kiss would change her mind?

Would it change her mind?

No. It wouldn't.

She shivered a little as Sean ran his hand up and down her bare arm, but she smiled in spite of everything. Because he had been right. It was important to play their parts.

"We'd like to thank you all for being with us today," Sean said, his voice like chocolate, rich and dark. "I know it means a lot to Melinda and to Walter to have you all here."

Another rousing cheer followed that little speech and as the music jumped into a rock and roll beat, Walter stepped out of the crowd and walked toward them. First, he offered his hand to Sean.

"Well said," he acknowledged with a shake and a nod. Then the older man turned to Melinda. "You are as lovely a bride as your mother was."

Tears filled her eyes again as she hugged her grandfather and breathed in his familiar scent of pipe tobacco and peppermint. He was the reason for this pretense and yet, she couldn't find it in her heart to blame him. He was doing what he thought best, just as he always had. Melinda only hoped that when this was all over, he would accept that she wouldn't be marrying again.

"I love you," she whispered and felt him drop a kiss to the top of her head.

"And I you. Now…why don't the two of you go and enjoy your party?" One last squeeze and he left her, strolling toward the corner of the grand ballroom where a few of his closest friends waited.

"He really is something else," Sean muttered.

Melinda looked up at him, ready to defend her grandfather—then she saw it wasn't necessary. Sean must have read the battle-ready light in her eyes though because he grinned.

"No offense intended," he said, holding up both hands in surrender. "I mean it. Might not like how he gets things done, but you've got to admire a man who goes after what he wants and doesn't take no for an answer."

In spite of her inner turmoil, Melinda smiled. "Of course you would admire him. You're a lot like him."

Both black eyebrows rose high on his forehead. "Is that a compliment or an insult?"

"Maybe a little of both."

"I can live with that," he told her, then steered her off the dance floor before they were crushed by the expanding crowd. Tucking her hand through his arm, he walked with her to a set of French doors and then stepped outside.

The cool breeze wafted over them both and Melinda drew her first easy breath in hours. It was good to get away from everyone for awhile. She looked back over her shoulder and watched all of the wedding guests dancing and laughing, and felt like an outsider at her own wedding.

"You're doing it again," Sean said softly.

"What?"

His strong, tanned fingers cupped her chin and gently turned her face to his. "Wasting time on regrets."

"That's not it."

"Then what?"

She took a breath, stepped free of him and walked to the edge of the balcony. On the other side of the railing, soft, outdoor lighting made golden puddles in the garden. The heavy scent of jasmine drifted to them and overhead, the moon was bright, dazzling in the sky. "I just thought that when I got married…"

"You'd be in love?"

She looked at him. "Well, yes."

"Understandable," he allowed and leaned one hip against the stone balustrade. "And you still can one day."

"No, this is it for me," she said with a shake of her head. "I'm not looking for love or romance. So, no more weddings."

"Funny," he murmured, "I said that once."

Surprised, she looked at him. "You were married before?"

Sean frowned and wished he could bite back those words. He hadn't meant to mention that first miserable marriage. Hell, he had never spoken of it—until now at precisely the wrong moment. What did that say? Was it a Freudian slip? Great. Now he was going to psychoanalyze himself. Good times.

Meanwhile, his new wife was staring up at him, waiting for an explanation, and he knew damn well he wasn't going to give her one.

Which would only make her more determined to uncover his secrets. One thing you could depend on with a woman, he mused silently, they had ways of worming information out of a man and they didn't usually give up until they'd succeeded.

Maybe he could avoid that by giving her a little without spilling his guts.

Shrugging, he said only, "It didn't take."

"So you're divorced."

"Not anymore," he said, giving her that half smile again. "As of now, I'm a married man."

Her mouth curved slightly in response, but the action never reached her eyes. "Yes. Married."

He turned and looked out at the garden and the moonlit ocean beyond. The soft wind ruffled his hair and teased at the edges of his jacket. "Don't sound as happy about our bargain as I thought you'd be.

"It's complicated."

"Didn't taste complicated to me," he said, turning his head to look at her.

Damn she was beautiful. He had thought that when he saw her walking down the aisle toward him that he would want to bolt. Instead, he'd stood there as if nailed to the floor. Unable to look away from the picture she made. That black hair falling over bare skin. The stark white gown that clung to her curves only to spill down around her legs in sensuous folds of silk. The swell of her breasts with each breath she took and the sheer, steely determination in her clear blue eyes. All of it had seemed *designed* to seduce him into staying right where he was—the perfect bridegroom looking at his future.

Their audience had sighed with appreciation when Melinda slid her hand into his and Sean could still feel the charge of heat he had felt when their palms brushed. Then dancing with her, *kissing* her had opened up a whole new world of hunger inside him and he was still trying to deal with the ramifications.

Standing with her in the moonlight wasn't helping the situation any, either.

She took a breath, blew it out and said, "Sean, about that kiss…"

Yeah, it was pretty much uppermost in his mind at the

moment, too. Well, that and the incredible hard-on it had caused. Damn, he hadn't reacted that fast to any other woman before. Just the feel of her body meshed to his had set him off and so far, the ache in his groin didn't show any signs of leaving.

Which meant that the next two sex-less months were going to be even harder than he had anticipated. He gritted his teeth at the thought, but couldn't bring himself to regret that kiss. If anything, he wanted more.

"It was a good one," he admitted, turning his back on the view so that he could study the woman he had married.

Moonlight caressed her skin and made the strapless white dress she wore almost glow with an otherworldly light. She was, in a word, breathtaking. He could hardly tear his eyes off of her.

The filmy material of her gown highlighted an amazing figure. Everything about her made him want to grab hold, pull her close and kiss her until neither one of them could draw a breath. And Sean had never really been known for his restraint.

It was taking everything in him not to touch her again. To feel that electrical charge of something amazing when their skin met. He wanted to slide his hands over her body until she was moaning and sighing in pleasure. His groin ached like a bad tooth and everything in him felt coiled and more than eager. If he had his way, he'd be taking his new bride upstairs to her suite, where they'd be living together for the duration.

He'd lay her down on the closest flat surface he could find, then he'd hitch the skirts of her dress up and stare down into her eyes as he pushed himself inside her. He'd feel her long legs wrap around his hips, pulling him higher, deeper. He'd watch her eyes glaze and listen to her panting breath and groaning sighs. He'd feel her slick heat surrounding him as he emptied himself inside her and then before the last of their climaxes had stopped rippling through them, he'd do it all over again.

"We can't do that again," she said, effectively snapping him right out of his private fantasies.

Scowling, he shifted position, trying to ease the pressure in his slacks a little. No good. Shaking his head, he tried to lighten the mood, softening the images still racing through his mind.

"Sure we can," Sean countered, moving a little closer to her. "Kissing's not sex."

"It is the way *you* do it," she murmured.

He grinned even as his body tightened further. "Flattery will get you everywhere."

"That wasn't a compliment."

"Could've fooled me," Sean said and stepped in front of her, putting her back against the railing. Her gaze darted to one side as if she didn't quite trust herself to look into his eyes. And Sean didn't want her uneasy. He wanted her soft and pliant and enthusiastic—as she had been during that amazing kiss.

His voice soft, his words careful, he said, "It was just a kiss, Melinda. It won't go anywhere else unless you want it to."

"I don't," she said immediately, turning her eyes back to his. "I can't."

"Then we won't go any further. But a kiss, Melinda, that's a safe zone. Just because we won't do anything else doesn't mean we can't enjoy ourselves a little."

She chewed at her bottom lip, indecision rife on her face.

"Maybe it wasn't as good as we think it was," he said, lifting one hand to trace the tips of his fingers along her jawline. "Maybe we were both just taken by surprise and read too much into it. Maybe we should test that theory."

"I don't think…"

"Good idea," he murmured, his gaze moving over her features like a starving man seeing a banquet spread out in front of him. "Don't think."

He bent and took her mouth again. This time he was hungrier than before because this time, he knew what he would find. Knew the taste of her, the feel of her. This time when she moved into him and parted her lips for his tongue, he was prepared for the jolt of heat that nearly staggered him.

He rushed toward the edge of his already tattered control. She was warm and luscious and her passion fired his own. Kissing her before had been a revelation. Kissing her this time was a confirmation of everything he had experienced earlier. The feel of her lips, the taste of her tongue, her sweet breath sighing into him all gathered into a tight ball of lust that seemed to grow with every passing second. He couldn't ease back, though he knew he should.

This hadn't been part of the deal. This instantaneous explosion of need was like nothing he had ever known before. If he had felt like this with anyone else, he'd have taken her to bed and kept her there until the heat between them burned out. But that wasn't an option and damned if he knew what to do about it.

While his body raged, firing into desire, his mind shouted for caution. Control. He had given his word. And he would keep it, he assured himself as he delved deeper into her mouth, taking all she offered, giving her all he had. But for now, this moment, he needed what they'd found together.

He jerked her in closer, his arms coming around her like steel bands. Her breasts pressed to his chest, he felt the wild racing of her heart and knew...*knew*...that she was feeling everything he was.

That knowledge gave him silent permission to feel more. He swept one hand to the zipper at the back of her gown and when she moaned into his mouth, he pulled that zipper down. An inch. Two inches. Just enough to loosen the bodice of her gown so that he could...

He gently lowered the top of her dress to bare her breasts. Then he tore his mouth from hers and bent to take first one pebbled, rose-colored nipple and then the other into his mouth.

She sucked in a gulp of air and shivered in reaction. Her voice was hardly more than a hush as she cried, "Sean!"

His chest tightened, his groin was so hard and heavy he winced from the pain, but didn't stop what he was doing. Couldn't stop. He reveled in her every gasp and sigh. Gloried in the taste and feel of her nipples in his mouth. He ran the edges of his teeth across those sensitive tips and felt her tremble.

Melinda's hands gripped his shoulders as she arched into him, offering him easier access. He took it. With one hand, he caressed and tweaked one nipple while his mouth and tongue and teeth tormented the other. He felt as though he could never touch her enough. Desire ratcheted up inside him. Hunger gnawed at him and his body ached for completion.

Moonlight played across her skin and the murmur of voices and the muted strains of music coming from the ballroom behind them became nothing more than a vaguely acknowledged distraction from what was most important. The heat sweeping from her body to his and back again.

Sean felt her sighs ripple through her and straight into him. She shivered, and he knew it was his touch, not the cool breeze, that was affecting her. Her fingers combed through his hair as she held his head to her breasts. Every gentle scrape of her nails against his scalp sent electrical buzzes through his brain, his body.

He'd never wanted any woman the way he wanted Melinda Stanford...*King*.

That thought jolted him out of the haze of desire fogging his mind. She was his wife. The wife he'd promised to leave the hell alone. And he was practically taking her here on a balcony with her damn grandfather in the next room.

Muffling a tight groan, he called on the self-control he had been honing all of his life and reluctantly pulled away from her. He straightened up and then reached behind her to zip up her dress. When he was finished, he caged her between his arms as he leaned on the balcony trying to catch his breath and convince his dick that it wasn't about to explode in frustration.

"Sean?"

He looked into her eyes, and they were glazed, confused and so damned sexy he wanted to throw away his own stupid sense of honor and do what they both wanted to do. But he wouldn't.

Not yet, anyway. Not until she'd released him from the damn vow.

Her hands dropped to his shoulders and held on as if she were unsure of her balance and standing alone. He understood that completely. His own legs were a little shaky, which was lowering to admit. Hell, he'd never been so... rattled by a woman.

"Sean, that was—"

"Melinda," he said, resting his forehead against hers, "a couple more minutes of this and..."

"Oh. *Oh*." She pulled in a long, shuddering breath and nodded slowly. "I can't believe we just—"

"Yeah well," he whispered with a rueful smile, "it's been a long day."

She laughed a little brokenly and the sound wrenched at something inside him. "I shouldn't have—I can't believe I let you—wanted you to—"

Sean eased back and cupped her face in his palms. "Melinda, it's no big deal." *Liar*, his brain shouted, but he ignored it. "We're married, right? We kissed. We—" He let her go, and shoved both hands through his hair. "Just, don't beat yourself up over it, okay?"

"Sean, there's something you should know."

He waited and a moment later, she spoke again.

"I was engaged once. My fiancé, Steven Hardesty, died in a car accident here on the island more than a year ago."

Her gaze was filled with regret, old pain and the shadows of guilt. Only a few seconds ago, desire had been churning through his veins like lava. In one flashing instant, it was gone. In the very next heartbeat, it was replaced by anger.

"Steven?"

She nodded miserably, letting her gaze slide away from his. "He died and I—"

"What?" Sean demanded, turning her face back to his. "Needed to find someone to scratch your itch?"

"What?"

"Why else am I here?"

"Oh please," she said, misery in her eyes sliding away to show him that she too had a temper. "You know exactly why you're here. We have a deal."

"Yeah?" He just looked at her. "Deal or not, you didn't seem to be giving much thought to good ol' Steven a minute ago."

"You—" Her jaw snapped shut on whatever else she might have said. She settled for giving him a glare that should have set fire to his hair.

"You said you weren't interested in romance. Why?" Sean demanded, keeping his voice low, ever mindful of the room full of wedding guests right behind them. "After Steven died you went into proverbial hiding? Tucked your heart into a box and buried it with him, is that it?"

"You don't understand," she countered and a flash of anger that matched his glittered briefly in her eyes.

"Oh, I understand more than you think," Sean told her. He fought the churning sense of outrage and anger, but damned if he could conquer it completely. He snorted in disbelief at this whole situation. Melinda had researched him. Seems he should have done some of that himself. "So it wasn't all a business deal at all. I'm a damn substitute for the late, great Steven."

"Don't talk about him like that."

"Why not?" Sean argued. "I'm his stand-in. Who better?"

She whipped her hair out of her face and glared up at him. "You're not a replacement for Steven. I told you I *loved* him."

Her vehemence hit him harder than it should have, he knew. But there was no denying what he was feeling. God, he was an idiot for walking into this so damn blindly. All he'd been able to think about was making the deal. Getting the land. Helping the Kings to win one more time.

If he'd known she was mourning some other guy, he never would have done this. It would have felt too messy to touch.

"I don't get why you're so upset," she muttered, scraping her hands up and down her arms as if chilled to the bone in the soft tropical breeze.

"I don't like being lied to. Or manipulated," Sean said flatly. "Call it a flaw."

"I didn't manipulate you," she snapped. "We had a deal. And no sex was part of it—yet just a minute ago, you had my breasts in your mouth, trying to manipulate me into bed. So who's the guilty one here?"

Okay, that he wasn't going to take. Sean had never tricked or forced a woman into his bed in his life. And he never would. Now his *wife* stood there looking down at him like an avenging angel of chastity? And he was supposed to feel what? *Guilty*?

"Oh, I don't think so, honey," he murmured, his voice as soft as his anger was hot. Reaching out for her, he trailed his fingertips along her arms and watched her involuntary shiver in response. "You can convince yourself of whatever you have to, but we both know there was no manipulation here. You liked my touch. You still *want* my touch…"

"No…"

"Oh yeah," Sean said, forcing a smile that cost him every ounce of will he possessed. "You do. A couple minutes ago, you were sighing and moaning and enjoying every touch and lick and—"

"Stop it."

Sean shook his head. "Not a chance. You want to pretend to yourself? Go ahead. But we *both* know that a couple more minutes of what we were doing and your whole no-sex vow would have been tossed out a window. I'm the one who stopped, remember? I'm the one who pulled back."

"I was just about to—"

"Forget it. Sell it to someone who doesn't have the imprint of your fingernails on his scalp."

She flushed and even in the pale wash of moonlight,

Sean saw her skin pinken. Embarrassment? Shame? *Regret*? Who the hell knew?

"You might want to pretend that you're not interested in living anymore," Sean said, bending low enough that his mouth was just a breath away from hers. "But your body didn't get the message. It's still alive and right now, it's hungering—just like mine is."

She lifted both hands and shoved at his chest. He stepped back in response—not because he had to but because he could see she needed the space. And hell, so did he.

"You're wrong."

"No," he said. "I'm really not. But you tell yourself whatever you have to."

Neither of them spoke and the sounds of the party seemed to grow to fill the tense silence between them. Finally, after what felt like a lifetime or two, Melinda said, "I don't think I can go back into the reception. I'm going to go up to the suite."

"Fine." Sean moved back to the balcony and hands on the rail, stared out at the moon-washed darkness.

"What are you going to do?" she asked.

He turned his head to look at her and as much as he hated to admit it, a part of him wanted to comfort her. She looked a little…lost. But he shut down his soft and cuddly side in favor of nursing his righteous indignation awhile longer. "I'm going to get a drink."

"I meant—" She broke off and blew out a breath. "I meant, will you still honor our deal? Will you be coming up to the suite?"

Up to the penthouse suite where they would both be staying for the length of their marriage. Living with her, being near her and not touching her. For one split second, he considered calling the whole damn thing off. But he was pissed, not stupid. And he didn't go back on his word. Not even when he was sorely tempted to.

"Yeah," he said, watching her with a jaundiced eye. She was beautiful but dangerous. Wounded but sneaky. After a second or two pause, he said, "No worries. I'll play my part, Melinda. I'll be every bit the husband *Steven* would have been."

Six

"He said *that*?" Kathy took a sip of her iced tea and reached for a cookie.

Melinda broke a cookie into tiny pieces and then broke those pieces into crumbs before she answered. It was two days since her wedding and she hadn't spoken to Sean beyond the vague "Good morning" since she'd left him on the balcony that night.

She was miserable and tired and confused, damn it.

She could still see the look in Sean's eyes when he spoke to her last. That flash of fury mingled with the remaining glitter of desire. And the worse part? She still wanted him.

"Yep," she finally said. "He'll be the husband Steven would have been. He was furious."

"Well, *duh.*"

Her gaze snapped up to her friend's. "Whose side are you on?"

"Yours, sweetie," Kathy soothed, patting her hand briefly. "But I can see why he was mad."

"Well, I don't." Melinda folded her arms over her chest and glowered quietly.

"Yeah, you can," Kathy said with a short laugh. "You lied to him."

"I didn't *lie*, exactly."

"You just didn't tell him about Steven."

"He didn't need to know." She shifted her gaze to the harbor where several fishing skiffs were headed back to shore. A few kids were running along the pier, laughing, throwing bread to seagulls. For Tesoro, life went on.

"Seems like he did," Kathy said and Melinda looked at her. "No man wants to think he's taking the place of some other guy. And please. A *King*?"

"Sean said the same thing, but he's not taking Steven's place. No one could."

Kathy sighed heavily, but Melinda ignored it. She'd never understood her friend's dislike of Steven and Kathy had never wanted to talk about it. Now, Melinda didn't care to understand. It didn't matter anymore. Steven was gone, and she was married to someone else.

"So, one thing you didn't tell me," Kathy said.

"What?"

"The big make-out scene on the balcony…how was it?"

"Good."

"Good?"

"Great," Melinda admitted with another long sigh. "Amazing. Incredible."

"Ah." Kathy smiled knowingly.

"Exactly! How can I feel that way about anyone else?"

"Honey." Kathy's voice was a little less patient now. "You're alive. Why shouldn't you *feel* alive?"

She shook her head and looked back at the water, letting her gaze soften, her vision blur until the scene before her became nothing more than a wash of indistinct color. She couldn't let herself feel anything for Sean.

That would mean that she had let Steven go, and she had promised herself that their love was forever. She couldn't turn her back on Steven's memories. No matter what Sean King made her feel. He would be gone in two months. Steven's memory would last forever. The only thing she could give her late fiancé now was her loyalty.

She owed him that, didn't she?

"Tell your grandfather I'll have those strawberries he likes by next weekend."

"I will, thanks Sallye," Melinda said, giving the woman behind the counter a smile.

This early in the morning, there were only a handful of people at the outdoor produce stand. Melinda knew most of them and nodded greetings as she wandered back out to the dirt track where her car was parked.

She stepped out from under the canvas ceiling into the sunlight and tipped her face up to the cloud-filled sky. Then she looked out across the coast road at the ocean. There were a few fishing boats, a couple of pleasure craft and seagulls wheeling and diving in the air, looking for breakfast.

"Just another day in paradise," she murmured with a wistful smile, wishing her heart didn't feel like a lead ball in the center of her chest.

She usually enjoyed being up this early. But being awake because you hadn't been able to fall asleep was a whole different thing. She hadn't slept more than two hours at a stretch since she got married. Glancing down at the ring on her left finger, she sighed as the stones winked at her in the morning light.

It wasn't supposed to have been like this, she thought. Her faux marriage should have been well, easy. Turns out, it was anything but.

During the days since the wedding, Melinda had just been going through the motions. In front of people, she played the happy newlywed. In private, she survived an uneasy truce with her new husband. Sean was painfully polite and distant, and she wished he'd just yell at her again. Then at least they'd be talking.

"Because your last talk went so well," she muttered.

She lifted her chin in silent defiance as the memory of her wedding night rushed into her mind. After leaving Sean on the balcony, she'd headed straight for the penthouse suite that had been hers since she left college. She had showered and changed into a nightgown and then had lain in bed…waiting.

Humiliating to admit now, but she had actually *hoped* that Sean would come to her that night. Had thought that after what they'd shared in the moonlight—even though it had ended badly—he wouldn't be able to stay away.

That he would be the one to break their vow so she could enjoy him and still maintain the illusion that she hadn't wanted him.

Because it *was* an illusion. Melinda sighed, looked out at the fishing boats as the rolling waves made them bounce and sway on the water. The truth was, she *did* want Sean. Badly. More than she would have thought possible. She could hardly believe it herself. She hadn't felt the slightest bit of interest in any man since Steven's death and she hadn't expected to feel anything for Sean. But oh boy, did she.

Lifting one hand to her mouth as if she could still feel the burn of his kiss, Melinda tried to reconcile what she was feeling with what she *knew*. She had loved Steven. She didn't love Sean. So how could she be on fire by simply *thinking* about the man? And how would she ever get through the next couple of months?

This shouldn't be happening. Wanting another man was a betrayal of what she'd had with Steven, wasn't it? Guilt ratcheted up another notch or two inside her.

She sighed and remembered that the morning after the wedding, she had found Sean sleeping on the too-short-for-him couch in the living room, his long legs hanging over the edge. He hadn't looked at all comfortable, but every night since, that's where he had slept.

"I'm not even sure if he's punishing me or himself," she mumbled.

But either way, it was working.

"Not exactly the picture of a happy bride."

She gasped as a deep, familiar voice spoke up from behind her. As if she'd conjured him with her thoughts, Melinda turned to look up at Sean. He was tanned and re-laxed and all too gorgeous. He wore a King Construction T-shirt, faded blue jeans that clung to his long, muscular legs and a pair of scuffed-up work boots that somehow just added to his appeal. His hair was wind-tossed and lying across his forehead and when he tipped his sunglasses down to look at her, his eyes were warm, but shadowed with fatigue.

If something didn't break in their relationship soon, they'd both be in comas.

"You look like you're thinking deep thoughts." Sean watched her, and she was glad he couldn't read her thoughts as easily as he could her expression.

"Not deep, just…thoughts."

"Uh-huh." Sean looked up and down the narrow coast road. They were three miles outside the village and the only other cars around were the few parked alongside Melinda's. When he turned his gaze back on her, he pointed out, "You were talking to yourself. Never a good sign."

Great. Now she had to try to remember if she'd said anything completely embarrassing. But looking into his eyes was making her mind go blank. Probably not a good thing.

"It's only bad if you answer your own questions—or is that laugh at your own jokes?" Oh God, she was babbling. But her stomach was spinning and her mouth was dry. Sean had hardly spoken to her in more than a week, so why was he here now? And why couldn't she calm down? She couldn't stay nervous with him for the next two months.

He took the cloth bag from her hand and peeked inside. "Fruit?" He looked at her and his mouth curved in that half smile of his. "They run out of food at the hotel?"

"No." She made a grab for the bag, but he swung it out of her reach. "I just like having fresh fruit in the house and it's silly to call room service if I want an orange."

"Good point." He took her arm and steered her toward the rental car he had been driving since he got to the island. "You know, my brother Rafe used to live in a hotel. For years. He dug the maid service and the twenty-four-seven room service. But he hasn't missed it at all since marrying Katie. They live in her little cottage down by the beach."

She was hurrying her steps to keep up with his much longer strides. "Sounds nice—Sean—"

"It is, but Rafe never can leave things alone. He's adding on to the cottage. Building a second story, punching out a wall into the backyard to add a family room, too. Adding all kinds of stuff. Making Katie nuts, of course."

"Sean—"

"That's how they met, actually," he said with a laugh,

"we redid her kitchen, and Rafe just never left. Good thing, too. She makes incredible cookies. I'll get her to send us some—"

Melinda didn't know what he was doing or where they were going so she dug her heels in until he stopped to look at her. "I don't need a ride home. My car's parked over there."

"Yeah, I know." He shrugged. "Saw it *and* you when I was driving past. Just leave the car. We'll get someone from the hotel to come pick it up."

Nothing from him for days and now he was practically kidnapping her. She threw a look behind her at the people and caught them staring after her fondly. No doubt the local gossips would be cooing over this, seeing it all as very romantic when in fact, Melinda had no idea at all what was going on.

"What are you doing, Sean?" she asked, walking beside him again, trying not to think about the heat of his hand on her bare skin. "Where are we going?"

He drew her around to the far side of the red convertible, opened the passenger door, ushered her inside, then dropped the bag of produce onto the backseat. Leaning both hands on the top of the door, he looked down at her and said, "Thought we could go out to the hotel site. You can show me around."

She frowned and saw her expression reflected back at her in his sunglasses. "You've seen it already, haven't you?"

"Not up close and personal," he told her, going around to the driver's side and getting in.

Melinda took a long look at him and that twist of longing inside her tightened a little in spite of her best efforts. But she squashed it a moment later. She should just accept his change in attitude. Just go with the flow here and pretend the last week of awkward silences had never happened. But she couldn't. She wanted to know *why* he was suddenly acting more like the Sean she had first met than the man he'd been since the wedding.

"Sean, what's going on?"

"Nothing." He shrugged and started the engine.

Before he could put the car in gear though, she reached out and laid one hand over his. He stilled, pulled his hand free and slowly turned his head to look at her. Dark glasses hid his eyes though, so she had no idea what he might be thinking. After a long minute, he said simply, "I just decided to get over it, okay?"

"Get over it?"

His mouth worked as if he were choosing his words carefully before letting them out. "Look, things got out of hand on our wedding night. We both said some things, and I figure we should let it go. Start over. Spend some time together. Get past this—whatever it is between us. Make the next two months easier on both of us."

She blew out a breath and smiled. "I'd like that. Until just now, I was actually thinking that maybe you were going to call the whole thing off," she confessed. "Back out of our deal completely."

He took off his glasses and looked directly into her eyes so she couldn't help but see the insult written in his gaze. "If you knew me better, you'd know I don't quit. I don't go back on my word once it's given."

"Okay," she said and watched as his expression softened. He might be quick to a temper, but it faded just as fast, she thought, and chalked it up as one more thing she'd discovered about her temporary husband.

"So," he said, offering his hand, "truce?"

She took it, her much smaller hand swallowed by his. Again, there was that delicious flash of heat that seemed to zip directly from his hand into the center of her chest. But ignoring that heat was the only way to deal with it, so she did. "Truce."

"Excellent!" He wiggled his eyebrows at her, slapped his glasses back on then turned, put on his seat belt and told her, "Buckle up."

He put the car in gear and pulled out of the lot, waving to the people at the produce stand as he went. Out on the coast road, the wind slapped at them, but Melinda loved it. Her hair whipped into her eyes, so she gathered it up in one fist and held it at the nape of her neck. She turned her face into the wind and inhaled the salty sea air and the thick, intoxicating scent of the flowering vines along the road. Pink and white and deep red flowers burst from a wall of greenery so thick you could hardly see past them to the hills beyond.

But she didn't need to see it to know what was there. Acres of farmland followed by miles of green, stands of ancient trees and, farther inland, waterfalls. This was her place in the world, and she knew every square inch of it.

Now that she and her husband had a new understanding, the weight of worry and anxiety slid off her shoulders and Melinda felt the best she had since the wedding. She turned her head to glance at him. Even in profile, Sean King looked amazing.

"I took a drive by the site last week," he shouted, to be heard over the wind, "but haven't had a chance to really check it out in person."

"What have you been doing all week?" she asked, and thought how odd it was that she didn't already know the answer to that question. But since they'd been avoiding each other, it wasn't all that surprising, was it?

He glanced at her. "Mostly I've been setting up an office at the hotel. I'm using one of the suites for now.

When construction starts, I'll find something more permanent."

The car followed the curve of the road and as they came up from behind a row of vine-covered hedges, a spectacular view of the ocean spread out in front of them. Whitecaps danced on the surface and, in the distance, a lone sailboat skimmed over the water.

"It really is beautiful here," he said.

"It is," she agreed, then turned to look at him. "But you live at the beach in California, don't you? You're used to views like this."

Sean smiled as he glanced from the view to the woman beside him and back to the road. "I live in Sunset Beach. Not far from Long Beach where my brothers live."

"Is it nice?"

He thought about that for a minute. He'd always liked his place, loved the beach community and the easygoing pace of life. And he had always believed that the view from his house couldn't be beat. Until he'd come here.

"Yeah, it is," he said, slowing the car down so he didn't have to shout to be heard. "Used to think that I had the best view in the world." He grinned and added, "You already know I live in a rehabbed water tower. It's so much higher than any of my neighbors, I can see for miles in any direction. The ocean at home, it's…tamer than here. With the jetties and the piers, by the time the water hits shore at home, all of the temper's been taken out of it. It just sort of whimpers ashore—except during a storm, of course."

She smiled at his description.

Sean shrugged and said, "Never bothered me before really, but seeing the ocean here…waves crashing. That color. Not really blue, not really green. And so damn clear." He shook his head. "Have to say, your view beats mine."

"That's nice to hear."

He glanced at her again and smiled. "Still, can't get decent Thai food here at one in the morning."

"True," she said, glancing out at the ocean. "But there are compensations."

"Good point." And not all of the compensations were centered on the lush beauty of the island. Melinda Stanford herself was pretty damned intriguing whether he wanted her to be or not. Sean shifted a quick look at her and his insides stirred again. Probably not a good thing, but there didn't seem to be much he could do about it.

His hands fisted on the steering wheel as he gave himself a stern talking-to. He had no intention of getting involved with Melinda. There was no future here. There was nothing beyond the duration of their two-month deal. Best to keep that thought uppermost in his mind.

But then, his mind wasn't giving him problems. His body, on the other hand, seemed to be in a constant state of painful frustration.

"Have you talked to your brothers since the wedding?"

His thoughts splintered at the sound of her voice, and he was grateful for the reprieve. And he wasn't an idiot, either. He heard the unspoken subtext all too clearly. She was wondering if he had told his brothers about what had happened between them. About the aborted wedding night. About the kiss that had been driving him nuts for days and the fact that they hadn't even been speaking since that night.

Right. Just the thought of telling his brothers *any* of what was really going on made him cringe. Rafe and Lucas had given him so much grief over getting married in the first place, the last thing he wanted to do was give them more ammunition to use to hammer at him.

Besides, Sean had had an epiphany late last night. Easy to do lots of thinking when you were trying to sleep on a torture rack called a couch. Damn thing was so short for him, the backs of his knees had permanent dents from hanging over the arm for hours at a stretch. But thinking time had helped him come to a decision about this temporary marriage.

He'd been married before, and it was a nightmare. His ex-wife had lied to him, used him, then walked off and, he told himself, good riddance. So Sean knew the whole love and happily ever after thing was a crock told to fools to give them something to cling to on lonely nights.

Melinda hadn't learned that.

Hell, she'd grown up in Brigadoon. Sunshiny, happy people living in a world filled with glorious sunsets, warm water and sweet-smelling flowers. Of *course* she'd believe that the late, lamented Steven was a saint. The man hadn't lived long enough to disabuse her of the notion. He hadn't been around to disappoint her. Or hurt her. He hadn't lived long enough for Melinda to learn the cold, hard truth.

There was no such thing as love.

Happily ever after only existed in books.

Instead, Melinda had been left behind holding onto memories that no doubt got prettier and prettier with the passage of time. She was being romantic and female, insisting on tucking her emotions away and burying them with Steven.

Well, Sean had decided that the least he could do for her while they were married was to wake her up. To make her live again. And no way could he do that when they weren't even speaking.

So he put his own anger at being lied to aside and decided to use what he was best at. Charm. Hell, there wasn't a woman alive Sean couldn't get around when he turned on the charm. And once he got past Melinda's defenses, she'd see that lust was a lot more substantial than "love." Lust, at least, was honest.

"No," he said finally when he realized she was still waiting for him to answer her question. "Well, I mean I've talked to them. *Not* talking to Rafe and Lucas about a job would be considered a felony in the King family."

"Oh." She turned her face away to look out at the ocean. He didn't have to see her features to know what she was thinking though. Tension fairly radiated off her body. Even the line of her jaw was tight enough that he knew she had to be clenching her teeth.

"*But*, I haven't told them anything about us."

"Really?" Her eyes were hopeful but wary when she turned her head to him. "Why?"

"None of their business, is it?" He steered around a hairpin curve in the road. "They're in California. We're here. And what happens between us," he added with a meaningful look at her, "*stays* with us…to borrow a phrase from the Vegas ad agency. Just relax, Melinda. It's a great day. We're at the beach. It's all good."

"Okay," she said softly. "I can do that."

He slid a glance at her and saw her ease back into her seat. Her features smoothed out and the tension around her mouth disappeared. Good, he thought. Already working. In no time at all, he'd have Melinda Stanford King eating out of his hand. Then he'd let *her* seduce *him,* and they could both enjoy this marriage as long as it lasted.

In a few more minutes, they were at the future hotel site and he was parking the convertible. Beside him, she still seemed a little tense. Well, he was going to take care of that.

"Come on," he said, "let's build a hotel."

She smiled at him, and Sean felt a quick jolt of…something. He didn't want to put a name to it. Didn't even really want to admit to it. Ignoring that feeling wouldn't make it go away but, for now anyway, he was going to give it a shot.

Clearing his mind of everything but the moment, he got out and waited while Melinda did the same. She came around the front of the car, giving him a great view. She looked amazing in a simple pair of white pants and a bright yellow T-shirt. Her sandals displayed toes painted a soft pink and when he lifted his gaze to hers, he smiled. He was glad when she smiled back.

He just naturally took her hand in his. That burst of heat he was almost getting used to happened again with that simple touch, but he paid no attention to that, either. Whatever it was that lay between them was only going to help him seduce her.

This was going to go Sean King's way or no way.

Seven

Sean looked around, taking in the whole place in one long gaze. Had to hand it to Rico, he thought. The man knew his stuff. This was the perfect spot for a luxury hotel. The land was crescent-shaped, with a wide, perfect beach and two spits of land that jutted into a sea that was simply an impossible blue. Sean could imagine the private cottages Rico wanted, sitting out on those points—private spots perfect for honeymooners.

He hoped those future newlyweds had a better time than he was having at the moment. A glance at his wife sent another jolt of need shooting through him. He kept control, though it wasn't pleasant. Sean wasn't used to wanting a woman and then being denied. Until now, the only other woman who had ever given him any trouble at all had been his ex. Figured he'd only have problems with the women he *married*.

Maybe it was karma, he told himself. Payback for never

letting women get too close. So the moment he did, it bit him in the ass.

Happy thoughts. He shut them down and turned his attention back to the moment at hand. Scanning the area, he looked from the beach to the land. It stretched out for acres, then sloped gently up into the knoll where he guessed Rico wanted his house built. There were banyan trees sprinkled across the property, with their weird root systems dropping down from heavy branches to support their weight. Thick stands of woods surrounded the area and flowering vines crept across the ground and over rocks.

The sun shone down on the whole scene like a blessing and Sean inhaled the flower-stained scent of the sea. In his mind's eye, he could see the resort, spreading out across the ground, wood and glass and bright, tropical colors. It was going to be a beauty.

"It's a great view," Melinda said, bringing him out of his imagination. He looked to see her turning her head to where an insanely white beach drifted down to the ocean. The waves rumbled into shore with a relentless rhythm that sounded like the heartbeat of the world.

"I haven't found a bad view on Tesoro yet," he mused, then turned his head back around and imagined the sprawl of the exclusive resort that would soon be standing here. "Though I think this is one of the best ones around."

"I do, too. Grandfather was going to build a house here for he and my grandmother." Her voice dropped to a whisper as she stared out at the sweep of lush green. "But she was killed in the same accident that killed my parents."

He frowned, thinking about the proud old man and how much he had lost in one fell swoop. No wonder he'd held on to this piece of land so staunchly. It meant something special to him. It was a place of dreams, Sean thought, looking at the land with a new eye.

For just a minute, he wondered what it must have been like for Walter Stanford, alone with a five-year-old grand-daughter to raise. It wouldn't have been easy. But as far as he could tell, Sean thought with another look at Melinda, the old guy had done a hell of a job. Except, of course, for that romantic streak Melinda carried around.

"I think he'll enjoy seeing your hotel go up here," she said, looking around as if seeing the land for the first time.

"Hope so." Sean squeezed her hand as he started walking, tugging her along behind him. "It's gonna be a hell of a place when we're done."

"When do you start work?"

"I've already talked to a couple of the guys at the local construction company…"

"Ah," she interrupted, taking the grassy expanse at a run beside him, "then you've met Tomin."

Sean laughed as he pulled her to a stop in the wide shade of the nearest tree. "Yeah. Quite a guy. Did you know he's the hereditary prince of Tesoro?"

Melinda chuckled and shook her head. "To hear him tell it, he's also the prince of Tobago and the rightful king of Hawaii."

"All of that and a carpenter, too," Sean said with a grin.

Melinda's eyes shone with laughter. "A man of many talents and too many stories."

"Yeah," he said as he pulled her closer to the tree trunk. "About that. Any interesting stories from your childhood you want to tell me?"

Melinda's eyes went wide and horrified. "He did *not* tell you about the banyan tree incident."

"Oh yeah, he did," Sean said, laughing at the appalled

expression in her eyes. "I'm thinking I should see that tree for myself. Maybe put up a plaque."

"A plaque?"

"Something small and tasteful," he teased, "and it can read, *Here on this spot, Melinda Stanford went skinny-dipping and got her leg stuck in a root and couldn't get out until her friend Kathy went for help.*"

Melinda smirked at him. "Something small, huh?"

He shrugged and winked. "*Smallish.*"

"I was fourteen," she told him.

"Ahh, but in my mind, you were a lot older."

"Sean…" She tried to tug her hand free of his, but he just held on tighter.

Melinda was fighting her own desires for him and damned if he was going to make it easier on her.

"Can't blame a man for what he thinks," he said lightly.

She stared up into his eyes as a long moment passed, then she said, "I suppose not."

"There, see? We're getting along great. No pressure, Melinda. No expectations."

Okay, that was a lie, he admitted silently. But she'd lied first. She hadn't mentioned the guy she was still pining for before she got Sean to marry her, temporarily or not. So if he let her think he was letting go of his desire for her, then that was fair, right?

As if trying to distance herself from both him and the sudden tension between them, she said, "I wasn't really skinny-dipping anyway. I was wearing underwear, thank God. While Kathy and I were climbing the tree, our clothes got swept out by the tide. As it was, I was mortified when she had to go get Tomin to rescue me."

Well, now the image in his mind was of Melinda, as she was now, wearing only a lacy bra and a thong—pink, in his imagination—sitting in a tree, smiling down at him. His blood pumped a little thicker, hotter.

"Banyan tree, huh?" He patted the heavy trunk beside them.

"What're you thinking now?" she asked, giving him a wary look.

He smiled. "You don't want to know."

"Probably not," she agreed, then changed the subject. "So, what else did Tomin, the big gossip, have to say?"

"Lots of things," Sean told her with a grin. "But don't worry, most of his chatter was about the island construction team. How good they are, how professional and how we'd be stupid not to use them."

"Well, he's right about that," Melinda said. "Though I bet he didn't mention that he and his five sons make up most of the crew."

"No, he didn't." Sean's smile got wider. "Doesn't matter though. Now I like him even more. He's standing with his family. Working for them. As a King, I can understand that better than most. We're all about family."

She leaned back against the banyan tree. "I always wanted a big family. Growing up an only child was lonely sometimes."

He planted one hand on the trunk over her head and leaned in. "Yeah, I get that. I grew up an only child, too."

She looked up at him. "Excuse me?"

He frowned to himself. Couldn't believe the stuff he was blurting out to her. Things he never talked about with anyone. But it was too late to pull the words back and she was staring at him, waiting for an explanation. So he kept it as brief and as light as possible.

"My brothers and I, we've all got different mothers." Her eyebrows went up. Yeah, he could see how it sounded. Hell, he'd grown up with the reality, and sometimes even he had a hard time believing it.

"My father Ben, he believed in spreading himself around," he said wryly. "He didn't marry any of the women he was involved with, but he managed to leave a son behind everywhere he went."

"No daughters?"

"Nope." Sean shrugged, bent down and picked up a rock. Turning toward the ocean, he swung his right arm back and threw it as far as he could. Then he watched for the splash. "At least, not as far as we know. Kings tend to run toward boys. Though a couple of my cousins have had girls recently."

"You have a lot of cousins?"

He snorted. "Can't throw a rock in California without hitting a King."

"Must be nice." She sounded almost wistful.

He thought about it for a second. "Yeah, it really is. Nice to have people who will watch your back no matter what." He paused, gave her a half smile and added, "Don't tell them I've been saying nice things about them though. They'll never let me forget it."

"Your secret's safe with me."

"Good to know." He looked from her to the banyan tree she was leaning against.

"What're you doing?" Melinda asked, coming up beside him.

"I'm trying to picture you stuck in a tree."

She snorted a laugh. "It didn't happen here. I was on the other side of the island."

"Uh-huh." Sean looked from her to the great old tree and back again.

"Sean…"

"Yep, gotta see this for myself." He picked her up, cradling her close to his chest.

"Sean, put me down."

He grinned at her. Damned if he didn't enjoy the feel of her body pressed in close to his. Looking down into her eyes, he saw the laughter there and that zip of something different shot through him again. He pushed that thought aside though. "I need a visual aid."

"Are you crazy?"

"Just curious." He grinned again, reached up and plunked her down on a thick branch. Instantly, she slapped her hands to the wind-worn wood to keep her balance while spearing him with a hard look.

"You are crazy."

"Nope, just wanted to be able to imagine you in this tree."

"Fine. Now get me down."

"Not done yet," he countered and laid his hands on her knees. She stilled and took a breath. He wondered if she was feeling the heat sliding back and forth between their bodies. Then he looked into her eyes and realized that yes, she felt it too.

Seconds ticked past while they stared at each other. She was nervous. He sensed that much. Good, he told himself. Nerves meant she wasn't as sure of herself as she pretended.

"Have you seen enough?" she asked.

"Not nearly," he told her, meaning it.

"Sean…"

"Do I make you nervous, Melinda?"

She took a breath. "Of course not."

"Liar." He said it with a smile, but he saw that single word hit her.

"Help me down, please."

Sunlight dappled through the branches. The thick green leaves surrounded her, dancing in the wind, and she looked like a damn nymph up there.

He set his hands at her waist and lifted her off the tree, setting her on her feet. But he didn't let her go. He indulged himself in the feel of her. In the heat flashing in her gaze. In the soft sigh of her breath.

She looked...smaller, somehow. More vulnerable. And he really didn't need to start thinking of her like that. It wasn't his job to protect her, was it? Because he couldn't seduce her and look out for her at the same time.

And he'd really rather seduce her.

He supposed that made him a supreme jerk, but Sean was willing to live with that. As long as it got him what he wanted—Melinda in his bed.

Several days later, Melinda watched Sean with Tomin and his sons and it was a revelation.

Sean King was one of the wealthiest men in the world. His family was famous and counted royalty among their friends. Yet, he stood here in boots, jeans and a T-shirt, talking to regular working guys as if he were one of them. She saw the easiness in his manner, the genuine smile, and she knew this wasn't an act. This was who he was.

She tried to picture Steven standing around laughing with Tomin and couldn't quite manage it. Steven had always been more interested in the finer things than in simple pleasures. He had always talked about when they got married and had her trust fund, how they would leave this island and travel where they could meet the "right" people. She hadn't liked the sound of it at the time any more than she did now. Tesoro was home. Would always be home. But Steven hadn't been happy here. Funny that she hadn't actually realized that before.

She frowned slightly at the disloyal thoughts. Steven had been the love of her life. She had been devastated when he died. She still missed him. It didn't matter that they hadn't agreed on everything.

"We can get started leveling the field," Sean said, his voice capturing her attention, "then by next week, we can map out the foundations."

Sunlight was bright, and the trade winds were blowing hard today. Sean's thick black hair was tousled, and Melinda was forced to curl her fingers into her palms to avoid the temptation of reaching up to smooth it back. Shaking her head again she gave herself a good talking-to. Reminding herself that she would never betray Steven's memory. That she wasn't interested in another man.

Her body wasn't listening.

"Sounds good." Tomin nodded as his practiced gaze swept the area. "I can bring in extra crews from one of the outer islands if we'll need them."

"We will," Sean promised. "This is going to be a huge job and when we're finished here, we'll be moving on to the ridge to build the house my cousin is designing."

"Good news for all of us, then," Tomin said with an eager grin. "What about the trees?" he asked. "You want us to take them all out when we're doing the level work?"

A whisper of regret slid through Melinda at the thought. Of course, she knew that they would have to tear down the old banyans to build the hotel but she hated thinking about it. They were so old. So...breathtaking. They were as much a part of the island as anything else and the thought of losing trees that were more than a century old broke her heart.

Of course, she thought, Steven would have chuckled at that. He'd always teased her, telling her she cared too much about things that didn't matter. She chewed at her bottom lip as she admitted silently she had always hated that.

"I don't think so."

She blinked in surprise at Sean's statement. He looked right at her as he added, "We'll build around the trees. Seems a shame to cut them down, doesn't it?"

"It does," Tomin agreed, not even realizing that Sean's focus was on Melinda. "But it's going to cost you, redoing some of the plans to accommodate the trees."

Sean shrugged. "Sometimes it's worth going an extra mile or two."

Melinda flushed and wondered if he was talking about the banyan trees? Or *her*? He'd been nothing but attentive for the last several days. She'd taken him around the island, introducing him to the residents. He'd charmed Kathy and her kids and when they had left her best friend's house, Kathy had given Melinda a smiling thumbs-up behind Sean's back. Everyone on Tesoro liked him. He played chess with her grandfather every afternoon and had the hotel staff eating out of his hand.

But with Melinda he was even *more* charming. He seemed to be touching her all the time. Taking her hand, draping an arm around her shoulders, brushing her hair back from her face. And every little touch was like a burning match thrown on to an unstable stack of kindling.

And now this.

He would save the banyan trees. Because of *her*. Looking into his eyes, she knew he was remembering being with her, lifting her onto the branch of the tree. That one, tension-filled moment in the sun-spattered shade. And something inside her turned over.

Honestly, she didn't know what to make of Sean King—which worried her a little. In the beginning, this had been all business. Now, she wasn't so sure. Now, she felt as though she really *had* married a stranger. None of the research she'd done on Sean had prepared her for his thoughtfulness. Generosity. Kindness.

Her gaze locked with his, and he gave her that half smile she was becoming way too fond of. Something sizzled in the air between them and Melinda knew she was on a slippery slope.

An instant later, their connection was broken as he turned back to Tomin and said, "So let's talk equipment. How are we stocked for big machinery on the island? My brothers will be getting a cargo ship out this time tomorrow. If we need specific things, I can arrange it."

Tomin clapped his hands together and rubbed them in keen anticipation. "Well now, let me tell you what I'm thinking."

Melinda walked behind the men, half listening to their conversation and half concentrating on the wayward thoughts careening through her mind.

"We'll need at least two front loaders with the large buckets," Sean told Rafe that afternoon in a conference call. "The guys here have a bulldozer and a forklift, but we'll need the scraper too and an extra forklift would probably be a good idea along with everything else."

"Got it." Rafe made notes, then looked back into the webcam. "We'll round up a couple of crews, offer them room and board, plus their pay for the duration of the job. Shouldn't be hard to get a lot of volunteers to sign up for work on a tropical island. So how's it going out there?"

"Not bad," Sean said, leaning back in his desk chair.

The hotel suite he had set up as a temporary office was roomy and efficient, but damn, he felt as if he spent every waking moment in the Stanford hotel. If he wasn't in this office, he was in the restaurant or the bar or, God help him, trying to sleep on that hideous couch in the suite he shared with Melinda, wondering what she was wearing to bed.

How pitiful was that?

"Yeah, you do a great job of selling that," Rafe said with a snort. "I really believe you."

Sean gave his brother a snide smile. Sarcasm. Another thing the King family was known for.

"Fine. Work's great. Everything else, not so much."

"Told you not to marry that woman," Rafe muttered.

A flicker of temper ignited inside Sean at hearing his brother call Melinda "that woman." He didn't ask himself why his protective instincts kicked in. He simply accepted it. "Just what I needed. I-told-you-so's are so helpful. Thanks."

Rafe blew out a breath and tapped his pen against his desktop. The sound was so clear, the action so familiar, that for a second or two, Sean could almost believe he was sitting in his brother's office at their headquarters in Long Beach. Though, if he *were* at home, things would be a lot simpler in his life.

There wouldn't be a Melinda making him insane, for one.

"So, I heard from Garrett." Rafe watched him, waiting for a reaction.

He didn't wait long.

Sean jolted forward in his chair. "What the hell kind of family loyalty is that? I talk to our cousin, and he talks to you?"

He had only called his cousin, Garrett King, the day before and already the word was out? Some security expert, he thought with a sneer. Garrett and his twin Griffin owned and ran the country's foremost security company, and in between working for the idle rich, spoiled celebrities and the occasional royal… they did jobs for the family. But Sean hadn't known about Garrett's whole unable-to-keep-his-trap-shut issues.

"Relax, he didn't come to me about you. I called him about having him look into a series of thefts at the warehouse."

Stunned, Sean stared at him. "Why haven't I heard about this? What? I'm on an island so I'm not a partner anymore?"

"That's not it, you idiot," Rafe muttered with a shake of his head. "Lucas and I just figured you had enough going on right now."

"Great," he said snidely. "Thanks for doing my thinking for me. What's this about?"

Rafe shrugged, but Sean could see the anger in his brother's eyes, belying that casual action. "Just what I said. Somebody's broken into our warehouse down at the harbor. Made off with a few things."

"And how much are these 'few things' worth?"

Rafe shoved one hand through his hair. "So far, we've lost about a hundred and fifty thousand dollars' worth of equipment."

"Damn it Rafe, you should've told me."

"Why?" his brother snapped. "You know who's doing it?"

"No, but I have a right to know what's happening to *our* business."

Sean might as well have been on Pluto, he thought. Being on the island put him out of the loop and away from the business he and his brothers had built up from nothing. He didn't like knowing that there were things happening that he couldn't help with. He didn't have a hell of a lot in his life *except* for his family. And it was irritating as hell to be shut out—even if it was well meant.

"Yeah, well…fine." Rafe snorted. "Excuse me for cutting you some slack while you're off in paradise. From now on, we'll keep you posted."

That was as close to an apology as he was going to get from Rafe. "Good."

"Now, about Garrett. You've got him looking into your *wife's* old boyfriend?"

Sean sighed. He had known Rafe wouldn't let that go. There wasn't a single member of the King family who knew when to butt the hell out. "Yeah. Call me curious. I want to know about this guy. Who he was. What he was. The way Melinda says his name, it's like he was a combo of Mother Teresa and a superhero."

"Pisses you off?"

"Damn straight," he admitted. But there was more to it than that, and that part, he kept to himself. He wanted to know how to fight the late, great Steven's memory. He wanted to be able to purge that guy from Melinda's mind, and to do that, he needed to know what he was fighting.

"You know, I wasn't going to tell you this," Rafe said, "but Lucas bet me a thousand dollars that you wouldn't last out this idiotic marriage."

Insult shot through him. "Hope you took the bet, because that'll be the easiest grand you ever made."

Rafe smiled. "I'm not an idiot, unlike our brother. See, I know that you *never* go back on your word. And, that you got the lion's share of stubbornness from Dad."

"Thanks, I think." Being compared to their father wasn't exactly a compliment, but good to know that at least one of his brothers had faith in him. "You can tell Lucas for me that I'm not going anywhere until the two months are up."

"I will," Rafe said with another grin. "He won't believe

it, but that's his problem. So now, why don't you tell me what *your* problem is?"

Irritated, Sean snapped, "Not looking for a father confessor here."

"Not offering. Just trying to help."

"Nothing you can do, Rafe." The only thing that was going to solve Sean's current and ongoing problem of aching groin and miserable temper, would be to finally get Melinda into bed. Under him. Over him. Surrounding him. Taking his body deep and holding him there...

"*Sean!*"

"What?" He shook his head and glared at Rafe. "What're you yelling at?"

"You zoned out. Care to tell me what you were thinking about?"

"No. Did you want to talk about Katie with us?"

"Good point. So, back to business then." Rafe checked his notes, read them back to Sean and asked, "That everything?"

Sean almost said yes, then reconsidered. "There is one more thing."

"Yeah?" Rafe listened as Sean talked, then smiled and said, "Consider it done."

"Excellent." Sean lifted his booted feet to the corner of his desk and crossed them at the ankles. "The cargo ship will leave tomorrow?"

"Should be in Tesoro by middle of next week." Rafe smiled. "Your other package will be overnighted to you this afternoon."

"'Preciate it."

"Okay then. We'll talk again in a couple of days. And Sean—" Rafe paused. "If you need anything, we're just a quick flight away."

"Thanks," he said, meaning it. No matter how irritating his brothers could be sometimes, it was good to know that they always had his back. Even if Lucas was dumb enough to bet against him. "I'll let you know."

He ended the connection, closed his laptop and turned in his chair to stare out at the amazing view stretched out in front of him. The ocean beckoned. The sunlight, the fresh air. If he didn't get out of this hotel soon, he was going to lose it.

But he could wait one more day.

As soon as his package arrived from home, he'd make his move.

Eight

It was a perfect day to be out on the water.

Melinda's hair was in a thick braid to keep it out of her eyes. She wore a bright red tank top and a pair of white shorts and sneakers to help keep her footing on deck. She came up from the shadows below, stepped into brilliant sunshine, then took a second to look out at the wide expanse surrounding them. On the left was the island. Everywhere else, the ocean. In the distance, thunderheads gathered on the horizon and promised a storm later. But for now, the day was just right, with the heat of the sun pouring down on them and the cool sea breeze cooling them off.

Slowly, she turned to watch Sean at the bridge. He looked right at home there, his big hands steady on the teak wheel, his cool blue eyes focused on the sea, and she wondered if there was anywhere Sean King *didn't* look as if he were in charge.

In this tropical setting though, his black jeans and black T-shirt made him look even more dangerous than he usually did. Which was really saying something. She took a deep breath and enjoyed the opportunity to really have a good, long look at him. With his back to her, he wouldn't see her admiring gaze and that was a good thing. He really didn't need to know that it was getting harder and harder for her to ignore the incredible rush of desire she felt for him.

Her stomach buzzed with the sensation of a million butterflies taking flight at once, and she realized she was almost used to that sensation by now. Melinda's gaze dropped, taking in his broad back, narrow hips and long legs. Then she saw he was barefoot and somehow, that was so damn sexy, she found herself struggling just to breathe. Her heartbeat quickened, and she was forced to swallow hard against the sudden knot in her throat.

Sean King was temptation on two legs.

This last week had been…amazing, really. After that afternoon at the construction site, they'd spent every day together. He'd made her laugh, asked her opinion on the hotel design and in general made her feel more important than she ever had. More…essential.

He listened to her when she talked, entertained her with his stories about his family and filled her dreams with images that left her waking up aching.

Guilt tugged at her insides as she realized that she'd never experienced any of those feelings with Steven. Different from Sean, Steven had been a *shallow* kind of man. God, she couldn't believe she was even thinking that, but if she had to be honest about it, that was the word for him. They'd never spoken about anything serious. Never talked about the future or what it held. It had all been in the moment.

Exciting and yet—

Sean turned his head, and his blue eyes locked on her. A slow half smile curved his mouth, and she swore she could feel the pull of him—as if he were simply drawing her into his orbit. There didn't seem to be any way to avoid it—and since she was in honesty mode—Melinda could admit to herself that she didn't want to. She enjoyed being with Sean. She relished the moments when he would reach out and touch her hand. Or smooth her hair back from her face. She'd gotten used to him being there. With her. At her side.

And suddenly the thought of this marriage ending in a few short weeks felt more like a death knell than a re-sounding bell of liberation.

"Serious thoughts?" he asked.

"No," she lied, with a shake of her head.

"Good." He nodded and gave her another of those smiles. "Too pretty a day to be wasted. Come on up here."

She pushed her earlier thoughts aside, told herself to get a grip and climbed the short ladder to the bridge. The *Corazon* was as familiar to her as her bedroom at the hotel. She'd practically grown up on the yacht. Her grandfather loved this ship. He never had been one for sailing—had claimed that he preferred speed to lolling around waiting for Heaven to give him a green light to go anywhere.

So the engine was powerful, the hull was sleek and they sliced through the crystalline waters like a hot knife through butter.

"It's a great boat," Sean said, turning the wheel to follow the curve of the island.

"Grandfather used to take me out on it all the time when I was a little girl. I always loved it."

"Not surprising," he said, keeping his gaze fixed on the ocean. She liked that about him too. The careful regard he showed for whatever he was doing at the moment. She liked his focus. His concentration. Especially when that laserlike focus was on *her*.

"Most people don't build boats like this anymore," he said, smoothing one hand across the gleaming wood dashboard. "They go for fiberglass or some damn thing." He flashed her a quick look and a grin. "Of course, my brother Decker has a company that builds, as he calls 'em, *real* boats. Luxury craft, like this. And man, Deck would love this beauty. It's damn sexy."

Oh, yes, she thought. Sexy was the word for it. Though she wasn't thinking about the boat at the moment.

She watched him as he expertly steered the ship into a tree-shaded cove on the far side of the island. He cut the engine and hit the button that dropped the anchor. A series of metallic clangs echoed briefly in the air as it dropped to the ocean floor.

When it was quiet again, the only sound the sigh of the water against the hull and birds in the nearby trees chirping crazily, she asked, "You're really good at handling boats. I know you said you live at the beach now, but did you grow up around the water too?"

He snorted. "Hardly. I grew up in Vegas." He turned toward her and leaned one hip against the wheel. "My mom was a showgirl at the Tropicana when my dad met her. For me, it was desert heat, the glow of neon and the sense of quiet desperation that hangs over the strip."

Surprised, she sat on a stool right beside him. The gentle rocking motion of the boat was a sensual motion that made her think of other, more primal rhythms. She cleared her mind and told herself to focus. "Funny, I never really thought of Las Vegas as anybody's *home*."

"It wasn't," he muttered, shifting his gaze to the trees

beyond the boat. "I just lived there. Until I was sixteen, anyway."

"Sixteen?"

"Had to leave," he said shortly. "Went and lived with my father until I left there for college and—"

"What?" She was watching him, waiting for him to finish his story, but his lips were clamped tightly together as if he were forcibly keeping the words from coming out. The sun pushed its way through the canopy of trees, tossing dappled shade across his face.

Finally, he blew out an exasperated breath and asked, "Why is it I find myself telling you things that I've never told anyone else?"

"Easier to talk to a stranger?"

One corner of his mouth went up. "We're not strangers, Melinda."

"I guess not," she said, realizing that she probably knew Sean better right now than she had known Steven. Though she'd promised to love *him*, forever. But then, time had nothing to do with feelings, did it? You could know someone for years and never really *know* them. Or, as with Sean, feel that instant attraction—that magnetic pull of one soul to another and—oh God, she was getting worse and worse.

"Maybe I've just got a friendly face?" Her quip was lighter than she felt, but she was trying to ease the tension within. It wasn't helping.

He just stared at her for several long, heart-stopping seconds. "You've got a gorgeous face. So, yeah. Maybe that's why. Maybe I'm just a sucker for a pretty face."

Now Melinda laughed. "I can't see you being a 'sucker' for anyone."

He snorted a humorless laugh. "You couldn't be more wrong, babe."

There was a world of old pain in those words. Shadows flickered in his eyes, and, instinctively, Melinda reached out for him, laying one hand on his forearm. He was always smiling. Always seemed so easygoing, that knowing something was haunting him bothered Melinda more than she would have cared to admit. "Sean? What is it?"

He glanced down at her hand on his arm, then frowned and took her hand in his. "Never mind me. What's this?"

The abrupt change in topic threw her for a minute. Her gaze fell to where his thumb was rubbing gently back and forth across a red mark on the back of her hand. "Oh, it's nothing. Just a little burn."

His gaze snapped to hers. "How'd you burn yourself?"

She shrugged. She hadn't even given that minor burn a thought. "Would you believe a soldering iron?"

"Not what I expected," he admitted, then softly drew his fingertips across the raised, red ridge.

It's just sensitive, Melinda assured herself silently. That's why Sean's touch was giving her goose bumps. It had nothing to do with Sean himself. Nothing at all to do with the swirl of heat mounting inside her. But even she didn't believe that.

"What were you soldering?"

She forced a smile and tugged her hand free of his. Every time he touched her, her brain seemed to go on vacation. And since they were alone together, Melinda needed every scrap of willpower she could command. And truth to tell, she didn't have much left when it came to Sean King.

Over the last week or so, he'd worn away most of her defenses as relentlessly as water on stone. She was hanging on by a thread and only her memories of Steven were keeping her from giving in to what her body was demanding.

Even now, her skin hummed with electricity from Sean's touch. Ignoring that buzz of sensation, she said lightly, "If you can keep secrets, so can I."

He nodded, as if accepting her at her word. "Okay, but I've also spilled a couple of secrets, too. So, I'm thinking you owe me one, and I'd really like to know how you hurt yourself."

His eyes were bright again. No hint of shadows as he looked at her. Just the banked desire that was always there, just beneath the surface. She was glad for it, but at the same time, she felt that dangerous quickening happening between them again. How was it possible to want someone and not *want* to want them all at once?

A question for the ages, she mused. And not one that was going to be answered anytime soon.

"When we get back to the hotel," she said, taking a step away, just for safety's sake, "I'll show you."

"*Show* me?" He closed the distance between them again and cupped her chin as he rubbed the pad of his thumb across her skin. "Nothing I like better than a good game of Show and Tell."

"I'll bet," she murmured and he must have heard her because his smile widened and he winked at her.

Oh, boy. She was in some very deep trouble here.

And Sean looked as if he was enjoying her nervousness. Though what man wouldn't? But instead of pushing her, crowding her, he backed off and a part of her wanted to whimper. Which was irritating as hell, Melinda thought. Was her body just refusing to get the message her mind kept sending?

"So," he said, heading for the steps, "good place for our picnic."

She watched him go. "Picnic? I thought we were out for a ride."

He paused on the steps, hands gripping the rails. A capricious wind caught his hair and tossed it into his eyes. He whipped his head back to clear his vision and his blue gaze locked with hers. "Nope. A nice picnic and I'm thinking maybe a swim."

"I didn't bring a bathing suit."

"Clothing optional," he said with another wink.

Melinda's blood bubbled and boiled in her veins. She knew it because she could actually *feel* it. Her heartbeat jumped into overdrive as she watched him climb down the steps then disappear below decks.

Skinny-dipping with Sean King? That would be a major error. She was already too tempted by him. Seeing him naked and wet and...her mind conjured up an image that made her knees go suddenly weak. Nope. She couldn't do it. He was her husband—but not. This was a marriage—but not. So sex was out of the question—or not?

Oh, God.

"Got a surprise for you," he called out as he stepped onto the deck.

She had already done a darn good job of imagining what his surprise was. She didn't think she could take too much more.

"What is it?"

He tipped his head back, looked up at her and challenged, "Come on down and see for yourself."

"Oh, that's okay. Think I'll stay up here for awhile." Yep. Safer that way. Keep some distance between them. Although, she was pretty much trapped on this boat with him and though she used to think of the yacht as huge, right now it felt like the size of a rowboat.

He looked up at her and grinned as if he knew exactly

what she was thinking. And he probably did. So, if she stayed up top like a big chicken, then he would know exactly how much he was getting to her.

"Okay," he said, his tone teasing as he opened a picnic hamper obviously prepared by the hotel chef. Reaching in, he pulled out a flat white box and lifted the lid. "But if you're up there, you can't have any of what my sister-in-law Katie sent us...."

Katie. The one he'd called the cookie queen. Curious, she edged closer to the rail and watched him as he reached in to pull out a single cookie. It was the size of his fist. White, drizzled with chocolate and even as she watched, powdered sugar drifted in tiny clouds to the deck at his feet.

"That's cheating," she said.

"I know," he countered and took a bite. His eyes closed, and he sighed as he chewed, an expression of pure bliss crossing his features. "She sent my favorites, God bless Katie King."

Her mouth watered and she was pretty sure the cookies had nothing to do with it. Just watching him was making Melinda want to drizzle *him* in chocolate and take a bite.

Oh, God...

"They're melt-in-your-mouth good," he coaxed, taking another bite. "Katie says they're called Mexican Wedding Cakes. But she tweaked the recipe a little, made them bigger and then she drips some melted dark chocolate on them when they're finished."

"Sounds fabulous," she said, easing toward the ladder.

"Taste even better," he assured her and opened his eyes to look directly into hers. "Katie's a goddess when it comes to cookies...."

She couldn't stop. She took one step, then another and before she knew it, she was standing directly in front of the man who was driving her absolutely out of her mind. "Are you going to share?"

"Everything," he assured her, but offered her the box of cookies as if he could take the sexual heat out of that one, single word.

Keeping her gaze fixed on his, Melinda picked up a cookie, took a bite and instantly felt the buttery, chocolate-swirled confection melt in her mouth. A sigh slipped from her throat before she could stop it, and Sean smiled and nodded in understanding.

"See? Did I tell you that Katie's a queen?"

"Maybe you should have married her." Melinda was getting a little tired of hearing how wondrously fabulous the great Katie King was. Even though, she had to admit, the woman's cookies were completely amazing.

"Rafe wouldn't have liked that much," Sean said, setting the box of cookies down on one of the blue leather bench seats. "Besides," he said as he turned to her, "I've got a wife."

Her breath hitched in her chest as Sean stepped closer to her. Heat poured off his body and reached for hers. But she was already feeling as though she was standing in the caldera of a raging volcano.

The tension that had been building between them for weeks now suddenly boiled up and spilled over. She'd tried so hard to stay true to Steven's memories, but Sean had chipped away at her distance, at her resolve, until nothing was left.

And maybe, she thought, she didn't *want* to resist anymore. Maybe she simply wanted to *be*. To feel. To release all of the pent-up pressure inside her. The look in his eyes told her that he was feeling everything she was and Melinda knew, without a doubt, that she was about to give in to what her body had been clamoring for the last several days.

Her mouth went dry and the cookie might as well have been made of sawdust. He plucked it from her fingers, and tossed it overboard. "Hey!"

"Give the fish a treat," he said, then bent his head to hers. "And speaking of treats..."

"Sean—" Call it one last-ditch effort to remember that pesky celibacy vow.

He stopped, stared into her eyes and whispered, "No thinking."

She nodded slowly and mentally let go of the threads holding her self-control together. "Good plan."

Every inch of her was quivering. He set his hands at her waist and pulled her in close, and she fought for air. Melinda was strung so tight, even her heartbeat felt thready. She'd been fighting her own instincts, her own urges, for so long now it should have been second nature.

But the truth was, she didn't want to fight against what she was feeling. What she *felt* for Sean. She wanted him more than she wanted air. She needed him to touch her, kiss her—and more. She wanted it all.

She needed it now.

The instant his mouth came down on hers, her brain shut down completely. There were too many sensations rocketing around her insides to allow a single, coherent thought. He parted her lips with his tongue and the quick, hard strokes he used to take her mouth only fed the fires engulfing her.

Her arms went around him, hands splayed on his back as she held him to her, closer. Closer. She met his kiss eagerly, their tongues tangled and twined together. Their breath met and collided, sliding from one to the other.

His hands swept up and down her back, sliding beneath

her tank top. He unhooked her bra with practiced ease, his nimble fingers making short work of the two tiny hook-and-eye closures. And then he eased away, sweeping her shirt up and over her head, her bra along with it.

The cool wind caressed her skin and she felt...deliciously wicked, standing in front of his admiring gaze. He lifted his hands to cup her breasts and his thumbs and fingers tweaked and pulled gently at her erect nipples until she moaned and swayed unsteadily on her feet. Tingles of awareness, anticipation, rippled through her. Melinda arched into him, her hands on his shoulders to steady herself as she let wave after wave of pleasure slide through her relentlessly.

"Beautiful," he whispered, gaze darkening with a passion that matched her own.

She wanted to feel his skin beneath her hands, touch him the way he was touching her, and she didn't want to wait another minute.

Tugging at the hem of his shirt, she muttered, "Take this off."

He did, yanking it over his head and tossing it to the deck in one quick move. She sighed as she slid her palms across a chest that was so tanned and well-defined, he could have been a statue created by some master sculptor. But he was real and warm and when she touched him, he hissed in a breath through clenched teeth. She smiled to know that he was as affected as she.

But her smile only lasted a moment before he was pulling her in close again, molding their bodies together until Melinda could feel the pounding of his heart against her chest. His mouth took hers, claiming her completely, and she gave herself up to the wonder of it.

Again and again, his tongue caressed hers, as he shifted his grip on her. One hand cupped her breast, fingers tugging at her nipple, while the other slid down to the snap and zipper of her shorts. He undid them, then moved his hand lower, across her abdomen to the juncture of her thighs.

A hot, aching need centered at her core and the moment he touched her, Melinda tore her mouth from his and gasped at the jolt of pleasure that shot through her. She had wanted so long, needed so long, that her nerve endings were electrified. The slightest touch would have her exploding in a release she knew would be shattering.

But he seemed to know that, too. Instead of caressing her most sensitive spot, sending her into the climax that hovered just out of reach, he dipped his hand lower until he could explore her depths. First one finger, then two, reached inside her, stroking, caressing the inner walls of her body until Melinda was parting her legs wider for him, rocking into his hand, helpless against the onslaught of sensations pulsing inside her.

"Come on, Melinda," he said, watching her through slitted eyes glazed with desire, "let go. Let me watch you go...."

"Sean—" She gasped his name, breathing hard, her vision blurred at the edges as she saw only him. Felt only what he was doing to her. The sunlight was too bright, the shade too dark and all around her, the world seemed to take a breath and hold it.

"Do it, Melinda." He dipped his head and kissed the line of her throat, nibbling at her pulse point, dragging his tongue along her skin.

She shivered in response and reached again for the release she felt coiled and clawing inside her. Her hands clutched at his shoulders as her hips moved in a rhythm that was fast and desperate. She locked her gaze with his, fired her emotions with the power of his. He rubbed his thumb across her core, and her body clenched around his hand. She felt her climax building, spiraling tighter and tighter inside her until at last, she cried out his name and lost herself in his pale blue eyes as her body splintered with a crashing release.

Breath heaved in and out of her lungs. Her legs buckled and threads of pleasure were still sliding through her when Sean picked her up and then laid her down on one of the cushioned benches on either side of the boat. The blue leather was warm against her back and she stretched languidly as she watched him peel the rest of his clothing off in a flash.

Her breath caught at the glorious sight of him. He was bigger, harder than she'd expected and that liquid heat at her core exploded in renewed anticipation. Lost to anything but the promise of more intense pleasure, she tugged at her shorts and panties, desperate to be free of them.

"You're killin' me," he muttered, that half smile firmly in place. He paused to grab his wallet and pull a condom from it before turning back to her. Locking his gaze with hers, he sheathed himself then reached for her.

"I want you inside me, Sean," she whispered, and she saw a flash of hunger dazzle his eyes briefly. "I need you."

"I know."

Melinda lifted her hips so he could tug her shorts and panties down the rest of the way, then she parted her thighs for him in silent invitation.

"Gotta have you," Sean whispered, his voice low and scratchy with the need driving him.

"Yes, Sean. Please, yes."

He covered her with his body, and she lifted her legs to draw him in. The tip of him brushed against her core, and Melinda groaned, arching and writhing, trying to get him inside where she wanted him.

But he held back, made her want. Made her crave.

His fingers moved over her center in slow circles, rubbing, caressing, until she was trembling from reawakened passion and a more consuming need.

She gulped at air, stared up at the wide sky above them and demanded, "Sean, inside me. Now."

"Almost," he ground out, and she knew that even as he pushed her higher and higher, the wait for completion was just as hard on him.

"You're making us *both* crazy, here," she told him, sparing a second to give him a heated glare.

"I know. But it's gonna be great."

Her hands rubbed over his chest, pausing to flick at his flat nipples with her thumbs. She heard his breath coming fast and furious, and she knew it wouldn't be much longer before he gave her what she wanted. Before he pushed himself inside her and took them both where they needed to be.

"Damn it, Melinda, I've been thinking about this moment nonstop for weeks now. I want to make it last."

"I've been thinking about it too," she admitted, "and I just *want* it."

He shook his head and gave her a hard look as she reached down between them to run her fingers over the sensitive tip of him.

He hissed in another breath and closed his eyes as if fighting for control. But she didn't want him controlled. Not now. Not when her decision had been made and they were finally where they wanted to be. She wanted him as frenzied as she felt. She wanted him to experience everything she was.

Looking up into his eyes, Melinda could hardly believe what she was feeling. She'd never known anything like this. Not with Steven. Not with anyone. Sean took her places she hadn't known existed. Made her soar higher and faster than she had ever been before. Only moments ago, she'd had the most shattering orgasm of her life and already she wanted another one.

And then another.

His touch. His kiss. His body against hers.

The water slapped against the hull of the boat. Birds sang in the trees, and the wind was a constant caress against her skin. It was a beautiful day.

And it was about to get even better.

Nine

Her fingers closed around him and he groaned, knowing he couldn't wait another second.

Caught in his own trap, Sean surrendered to the inevitable and pushed himself into Melinda's welcoming heat. And with that first, intimate slide of their bodies, he was lost.

Watching her pleasure as he took her only fed his own. Looking into her eyes and seeing them glaze over with passion spiked something inside him he'd never known before. He couldn't identify it—wouldn't even try.

Her legs wrapped around his waist, she hooked her ankles at the small of his back, pulling him deeper, higher. He looked down at her and watched satisfaction, chased by hunger play across her features.

Something fisted around his heart, but he ignored it. This was about sex. Passion. *Lust.*

This he knew something about.

This was what he'd been urging Melinda toward for weeks. This moment when she released her past and roared back to life. And he wouldn't waste a minute of it in self-reflection.

He sat back on his heels, drawing her up with him. Their bodies still locked tightly together, he held onto her hips and guided her as she began to move on him. Her breath came in short, hard gasps. Her eyes were fixed with his as she twisted atop him, making him feel so much more than he ever had before.

She threw her head back and laughed. "Sean. This. Is. So. Good."

"Damn straight," he muttered thickly, dipping his head to nip at one of her nipples.

She groaned and moved faster, harder atop him.

"Take me, Melinda," he urged through gritted teeth. "Take all of me."

"Yes. Yes." She increased the rhythm, and his grip on her hips tightened, helping her move, maintaining that synchronicity that was singing between them.

He felt the first shuddering explosion grab her, and, as she gave herself up to it, her body tightened around his, pushing him over the edge. His body erupted into hers, and the sound of her voice shouting his name was the best thing he'd ever heard.

Her hips moved reflexively and he went with her, riding that pleasure wave together until, finally, they clung to each other in the shattering aftermath.

Minutes later, they were still there, on the bench, bodies joined, each of them trying to even out their breathing. Melinda's forehead rested on his shoulder, and Sean swiped his hands up and down her back. His heart was racing and he was pretty sure his brain had melted.

Wrapping his arms around her, he silently marveled at the fact that this one small, curvy woman had knocked him right off balance. She had completely blindsided him, and Sean couldn't even make sense of the jumbled thoughts churning through his still-buzzing mind.

The sigh of her breath touched something inside him. As unprepared as he was for the sensation, he knew he had to say *something*, to break up this little tableau.

Finally, he blurted out, "I must have been a bastard in a previous life."

"What?" She jerked her head up to look at him in confusion.

He shrugged. "It's the only way to explain how I keep ending up on sofas and benches that are too short and too damn narrow."

Melinda just stared at him for a long second or two, then a short laugh shot from her throat and he felt it all the way down to their joining. He gritted his teeth as his body leaped into life again, then narrowed his eyes on her. "What are you laughing at?"

"Sorry, sorry." She shook her head and admitted, "It's just that the first time I saw you on the couch in our suite, I felt so bad for you, but…"

"*But?*"

"Well," she said, still smiling, "you looked so funny. Your legs hanging over the edge, your feet sticking out from under the blanket."

Subtext, he told himself with an inner smile, she had watched him sleeping. That was excellent news that he would think more about later.

For now, he gave her a mocking glare. This was good. He had wanted her thinking only about him. There were no painful memories crowding around her. No thoughts of

Steven encroaching on them. Here and now, it was just the two of them. So he did what he could to keep it that way.

"Thought I looked funny on that miserable excuse for furniture that you call a couch, huh?" He lifted her off of his lap, though he missed the feel of her body joined with his. "You know what I think is really funny?"

He stood up, swung her into his arms and she looked up at him with wide eyes. "Sean…"

He carried her to the edge of the boat. "I said something about a swim, didn't I?"

"Come on, cut it out." Her legs kicked, and she pushed ineffectually at his chest in a futile attempt to get free. She flashed a look at the crystal-clear water below her then back to him again. "Sean, you wouldn't…"

"Sure I would." He paid no attention to the way she was squirming in his arms. "Now, now, watch how you're kicking," he warned. "Don't want to hurt anything we might need later."

She laughed. "If you do what I think you're going to do, we won't be needing anything later…."

Sean gave her a wounded look. "Now see, that's just mean."

"You nut," she said laughing, "put me down."

"I don't think so," he continued, paying no attention to the way she was squirming in his arms, "we've got the 'skinny' part handled. Now all we need is the 'dipping.'"

And he dropped her.

Her shriek was cut off when she hit the water and went below the surface. He was watching when she bobbed right back up, pushing her hair out of her eyes and sputtering up at him. "You rotten, no-good, sneaky—"

He jumped in right beside her. The water was cool and clear. He opened his eyes underwater and got a great view of Melinda's amazing body before he kicked out and shot to the surface.

"You rat," she shouted and slapped a small wall of water into his face with the flat of her hand.

He ignored that, reached for her and yanked her in close. Then he kissed her, cutting her rant off midstream. She didn't seem to mind though, as she wrapped her arms around his neck and kicked her legs in time with his to keep them afloat.

When he finally pulled back, he looked into her eyes and whispered, "The only thing better than dry sex? *Wet* sex."

She leaned in, nipped at his bottom lip and whispered, "Prove it."

Sean grinned. "I love convincing a skeptic."

He headed close enough to shore that they could stand, but the clear, beautiful water was still deep enough to tease the tops of her breasts. Then he slid his hands down her slick body, loving the sighs that slipped from her throat.

He cupped her center, and she moved against him, parting her thighs for him, giving him easier access. Her eyes closed and a smile curved her mouth as he stroked her. Sean's own heartbeat thudded painfully in his chest as he watched her ride another wave of pleasure. And when she called his name, he took her mouth again, swallowing that sound and all the others that would follow.

Yeah, he thought wryly, just before his mind shut down, caught in his own trap.

"This is where you burned yourself?" Sean asked an hour later as they stood in the hallway outside a junior suite at the hotel. "What? You a closet arsonist?"

Melinda smiled and shook her head. It was weird, but she'd never felt so tired and so wired all at the same time before. They had spent most of the day out on the water, and just thinking about what they'd done had her stifling a sigh of satisfaction. If that storm hadn't blown in, she thought wistfully, they might have still been out there.

"No, not an arsonist," she said on a laugh. Melinda swiped her key card then turned the knob and opened the door to her workroom.

She had never invited anyone into what she thought of as her own private space before. Sean was the first. Ever. Not even Steven had been here. But then, he had never shown any interest in seeing it. Frowning, she realized that Steven had never really even wanted to hear about what she was doing. Or working on.

And *why* was she suddenly having all of these negative thoughts about the man she had been planning to marry? Then she thought briefly about the day she had just spent with Sean, and a tingle of guilt zipped through her. Shaking her head, she stepped into the room, hit the light switch and moved back so Sean could walk past her.

In the middle of the room, he stopped short and did a slow, amazed turn, gaze sweeping across the worktables, the bowls of gems and the glass case filled with finished pieces. "What the—"

"I make jewelry," she said, closing the door and walking to where her latest designs were tucked safely away.

"Yeah," he said on a laugh. "I guess you do."

He followed her and waited while she opened the case and drew out a velvet-covered pallet filled with jewelry she had designed and created right here in this room.

"I work with gold and sterling silver mostly," she was saying as Sean picked up first a ring, then a pin in the shape of a butterfly. When he moved on to a necklace made of slender threads of gold and topazes draped to hang like tears, she said, "That one is a gift for Kathy's birthday."

"It's incredible," he said, lifting his gaze to hers.

"Thank you." A real smile split her face as she read the sincerity in his gaze. She pulled out another tray of rings and said, "These are destined for the jewelry shop in town. I sell them there."

"You sell—" he stopped, reached across the glass case and caught her left hand in his. Rubbing his thumb across the wedding band he had given her, he asked with a chuckle, "So basically, I bought you a ring that you made."

"Well, yes." She looked down at her hand in his. "And you couldn't have pleased me more. You bought it because you liked it."

"It's beautiful, that's why."

"Well, you have great taste," she said with a quick smile.

"Yeah," he agreed. "I think so."

He released her hand, and Melinda missed his touch. She watched him look around the rest of the room. "You do amazing work, Melinda. But you sell your stuff way too cheaply. You're an artist. You should be famous. Selling to Tiffany or something."

Melinda laughed and felt a swell of pride. Except for Kathy, no one had ever really complimented her work. Sure, she knew it was good. James Noble never had any trouble selling the pieces she took to him. But somehow it was different, and meant more, hearing Sean calling her an artist.

As she put the trays back in the glass case and closed the doors, she said, "That's one of the reasons I wanted my trust fund so badly. I want to try to expand. Get myself a real workshop set up here on the island. Maybe find a contact or two through our guests and do what I can to get my jewelry some recognition."

He shook his head as he inspected the neatly laid out and well-organized worktables. "I don't get it. Why is your stuff only sold in the one store in town? If nothing else, your grandfather could carry it in the hotel gift shop."

Melinda shrugged sadly. "Grandfather doesn't entirely approve of me working."

"Ah." He nodded.

"He's old-fashioned—hence the whole get-married-and-be-safe thing. But in his defense," she said, "I think he was also worried that my work wouldn't be good enough. That I'd try to sell my stuff and fail and be hurt by rejection."

"No chance of that," Sean murmured.

"I hate to keep saying thank you, but—"

He cut her off with a quick change of subject. "So now that we're married, you'll get the trust fund and what? Leave Tesoro? Move to the big city and take up jewelry design full-time?"

"No." She shook her head firmly. That's the one thing she was absolutely sure of. "I don't want to leave. This is home. And, after all, it *is* the only place in the world that I can get the Tesoro Topaz."

"There is that." He looked around again before turning his gaze back to her. "So basically, the trust fund is freedom to follow your own heart. Do what you want to do most."

"Exactly."

"Then it was worth getting married," Sean said with a slow smile.

"I'd say so." Something inside her spun and trembled as he walked toward her with lazy, measured steps.

When he was beside her, he lifted her hand, looked

at the burn and asked, "Want me to kiss it and make it better?"

The look in his eyes promised more of what they'd shared earlier on the boat. She shouldn't want him again. Her body should be sated and happy and perfectly content. Yet, there was still a hunger inside her that she suddenly feared would never really be gone.

Just a few more weeks and this marriage would be over. She'd have her trust fund. Her business. She'd be independent and on her own and why did that all sound so... lonely?

Sean was smiling down at her, his arm snaking around her waist, pulling her close, and Melinda made a conscious decision to stop thinking about the future. To accept today and revel in it.

The truth was, there was nothing she wanted more than to christen her workshop with the birth of memories that would be with her long after Sean had gone back to his own life.

Dinner with her grandfather went well.

Of course, Sean had a hell of a time tearing his gaze away from Melinda long enough to concentrate on what Walter had to say. But then he had caught the older man looking at him with a knowing smile, and he figured Walter understood exactly what Sean was feeling.

Too bad he had the wrong idea about all of this.

Walter didn't know that this was all temporary. That the marriage was a sham. There he sat, pleased for his granddaughter and all the while, Sean felt like some kind of rat-snake for deliberately lying to the man.

He gritted his teeth and told himself silently to suck it up. He had voluntarily signed on for this little game, and he didn't have the right to bitch about it now. But it went against the grain, damned if it didn't.

He shifted another look at Melinda, and she smiled at him from her end of the table. A curl of heat whipped through his belly, and Sean's mind instantly dredged up an image of him and Melinda, naked in the crystalline water, with nothing but the sand and the sea for miles around.

And just like that, he was ready to toss her over his shoulder and carry her to the nearest bed. He smirked a little at the realization that the one place he *hadn't* had Melinda was a damn bed. Though the boat, he told himself, had been an amazing experience.

"What did you think of the boat?" Walter asked suddenly and Sean jolted—grateful as hell the old man couldn't read minds.

"It's a beauty." Sean took a sip of his after-dinner coffee. "I can't remember ever having that much fun on the water before."

Melinda flushed. In the candlelight, she looked luminous, and Sean smiled a little watching her embarrassment.

"Glad to hear it," Walter said. "I don't get out on the boat much anymore. I'm happy to know you're getting some use out of it."

"Thanks. I'd like to take her out again soon."

"Anytime," Walter assured him.

Melinda took a long drink of her wine.

Smiling, Sean said, "I spoke with my brothers the other day. The cargo and some of our crew will be arriving next week. We'll be ready to start on the hotel construction soon."

"Wonderful." Walter nodded thoughtfully. "A lot of people on Tesoro are excited about it."

"What about you, Walter?" Sean asked quietly. "How do you feel about it?"

The older man took a long breath and thought about it for a moment or two. Then he smiled. "I'm looking forward to it. Change can be a good thing. Keeps a man young. Interested in the world around him."

"You'll always be young, Grandfather." Melinda reached out and squeezed his hand.

"Hah!" Walter winked at Sean. "See that? How she sneaks into my heart so easily? She's always known exactly what to say." He lifted her hand and kissed it. Noticing the burn, he frowned. "You are not being careful, Corazon."

"Corazon?" Sean asked. "That's the name of your boat."

"So it is. It means 'heart' in Spanish and that is what Melinda is to me. My heart." Fixing his steely gaze on her, he added, "And when she is not being careful, she worries me."

"Me, too." Sean looked at her and saw her scowl briefly.

"So the two of you are going to gang up on me?"

"That's what family's for," Sean said.

"Hmm."

"She's shown you her workroom?" Walter asked.

"She did. This afternoon." Sean looked at her. "She does incredibly beautiful work."

"It's a nice hobby," Walter agreed pleasantly.

Melinda rolled her eyes, and Sean hid a smile. Odd that despite the fact that the older man loved his granddaughter deeply, he had no idea what was in her heart. Her soul. That he could dismiss artistry as a "hobby" was insulting. But clearly, neither Walter nor Melinda saw it like that.

"Oh," the man said, "I meant to tell you this before. If you need a place for your workmen to stay, I have another, smaller hotel not far from here. It's not fancy, but I'm sure your men would be comfortable."

"We appreciate that," Sean said. "Melinda was telling me that you once thought to build on that lot."

"I did." The older man sat back in his chair and lifted his coffee cup. "But when I lost my wife and Melinda's parents, I decided to stay in the hotel. A man raising a child alone needs all the help he can get, I'm not ashamed to say." He glanced at Melinda, and she gave her grandfather a smile. "She was treated like a princess by everyone here."

"I can see why."

Walter gave Sean a proud smile. "I'm glad you see what I do when I look at her."

He saw all of that and a lot more, Sean thought. Which was beginning to worry him. Somehow, the seduction of Melinda was working in the opposite way, too. *He* was being seduced right along with her, and he was going to have to find a way to pull back.

Or the end of this temporary marriage could get very messy.

"Okay, that's enough of the wonders of Melinda stories," she announced suddenly and stood up. "I'm going upstairs. You two behave yourselves."

"You do look tired," her grandfather said. "Probably too much sun."

She flicked Sean a glance. "Yes, that's probably it."

And all of the sex, Sean thought.

He watched her go and as she left the room, Walter leaned over and said, "She's a beauty, isn't she?"

"Yeah. Yeah, she is." Sean looked over at the older man. "But she doesn't know your hotel's in trouble, does she?"

Walter pursed his lips, tapped his fingers against the

table and finally heaved a long sigh. "You're too clever, Sean. How did you guess?"

"Little things," he said quietly. "Chipped paint. Frayed drapes. The bar's understaffed and the main dining room only serves lunch and dinner. When a business starts making cuts, letting the small things slide, there's usually a reason."

Nodding, Walter smiled ruefully. "So there is. But to answer your earlier question, no. Melinda doesn't know. And now that you have guessed the truth, I will expect you to keep my secret."

Sean didn't get that. This family had more secrets going on. Melinda wouldn't let her grandfather know about the marriage deal. He didn't want her to know that he needed money. She didn't talk about Steven and the old man seemed no different.

Way different than his family, boy. With the Kings, there were almost never secrets because no one shut up long enough to keep one. It was much easier to just argue about what was bugging you, get it out in the open, maybe punch your brother in the face and then let it all go.

Of course, Sean thought, he had been keeping a secret from his brothers for years. His first marriage. And suddenly, he wondered why the hell he hadn't told them. To save himself embarrassment? To avoid the shouting? Stupid to keep things from family. Especially *his* family.

"No disrespect intended, Walter," Sean said carefully. "But lying to her? Not the best idea."

"Ah," the older man said with a wink. "Soon, there will be no reason for lies of any kind. The sale of that land to your family will take care of the problem. I'll be remodeling the hotel—can't have your cousin getting *all* of the new guests—and there'll be nothing to tell Melinda."

"I sort of thought you might want to retire," Sean said,

surprised at the old man's willingness to stay in the hotel game and battle the Kings for guests.

"Retire?" His eyes widened in surprise. "That's for old people. What would I do all day? No. You'll see. My way is better. Melinda will get her trust fund, the hotel will be remodeled and everyone will live happily ever after."

"Here in Brigadoon," Sean muttered.

"What was that?"

"Nothing," Sean said and listened as Walter talked about his plans for the remodel. But even as the old man spoke, Sean's mind was upstairs with Melinda.

These last couple of weeks with her had been great. And today...put a whole new spin on the word *amazing*. But this marriage had an expiration date and it was fast coming up.

Which left him to wonder what the hell he was going to do when their time together was over and he was still on the island taking care of business. Were they just supposed to nod and smile at each other as they passed on the street? Was he supposed to pretend he didn't want her?

Walter's voice became nothing more than a buzz in Sean's mind. Background noise for the thoughts tumbling through his brain. He was getting wound up tighter and tighter in Melinda's life. Her world.

This hadn't been part of the plan. He didn't belong here on Tesoro. His life was back in California. His home was there. His family. This tiny tropical island wasn't the real world. Not for him. Melinda wasn't for him either. He knew that.

And yet...

This was getting more and more complicated, and

the worst part was, his brothers had been right. He never should have gone along with Melinda's scheme.

Because now that he was in, he wasn't sure he wanted out.

Ten

Sean left Walter a half hour later and took the elevator to the penthouse. His insides were twisted into knots and he couldn't form a single, coherent thought, but one thing came through loud and clear.

He wanted to see Melinda. Be with her.

For as long as he could.

Upstairs, Sean looked forward to finally getting off that damned sofa and sleeping in a bed. With Melinda. It had been a hell of a long day, and he should be beat. But the truth was, he felt charged. Just being around her made him feel more…alive than he ever had before. And if he was smart, he'd be worried about that, he thought. Instead, he looked forward to touching her again.

He heard her sobs the moment he opened the door. Panic grabbed the base of his throat. He slammed the door and followed the heartbreaking sounds of her crying. He'd never been in her bedroom and hardly noticed it now. All he saw was moonlight sliding through the open curtains and Melinda, sitting on the floor. Back against the bed, knees drawn up to her chest, she was staring at a framed photograph and crying as if her heart was broken.

Everything in him tightened into a hot ball of protective instinct that flashed inside him like lightning. Her tears were like a knife in his chest, pain ripped at him. In the space of a split second, he'd gone from a self-satisfied male about to get lucky to a man desperate to find whoever was making Melinda cry and beat the crap out of him.

Sean stalked across the room in a few long strides, went down on one knee beside her and said, "What is it? What's wrong, Melinda?"

She shook her head violently. Tears still poured from her beautiful eyes and her mouth was screwed up tight as if she were biting back the urge to wail.

He cupped her face in his palms and turned it up to him. "Talk to me. Tell me what's happened."

"I shouldn't have," she said and gulped in a breath. "I didn't mean to. But I did and now…"

"What're you talking about?" He looked at the photo she held so tightly and guessed instantly what was going on. The smiling face of a handsome man with too many teeth looked back at him, and Sean knew without a doubt that *this* was Steven.

Frustrated by his inability to fix this, he blew out a breath and muttered, "Damn it, Melinda, don't do this to yourself."

"How can I not? I was going to marry him," she said, her voice a painful hush that scraped at his heart. "I *loved* him and today I—"

"Melinda—"

"No," she shook her head again, clearly furious with

herself. "It's like I cheated on him. Not just because of the sex but because I *enjoyed* it."

Those protective instincts that had sent him racing to her side reared up inside him, stronger than ever, and put a stranglehold on the frustration pumping through him. He hated seeing her like this. Hated knowing that he'd pushed her here. That his plan to seduce her had left her feeling such misery.

Guilt was an ugly emotion. No one knew that better than Sean, he thought grimly. But this wasn't about him. This was about Melinda, and damned if he'd let her regret what had happened between them.

"It's okay to feel, Melinda," he said softly, shifting to sit beside her. "You're alive. You're *supposed* to live."

She sighed heavily. "You don't understand."

"Oh, I understand plenty. I know all about guilt," he said softly, dropping one arm around her shoulders and pulling her close to his side. She resisted at first, then slowly crumpled into him. He rubbed her upper arm in slow, comforting strokes. "Guilt will kill you an inch at a time until there's nothing left of you, Melinda. It's not worth it."

"Tell me." Her voice was a whisper against the curve of his neck. She cuddled closer as if needing the contact, and if Sean was going to tell this story, then he figured he'd need it too.

It was something he hadn't thought about in years. Purposefully. And it was a story he had told only to his father. So once again, he thought, he was sharing things with Melinda that he never shared with anyone.

"You know how I said I lived in Vegas until I was sixteen?"

She nodded.

"That's because at sixteen," he said, in a voice detached

from feeling, "I was finally big enough, strong enough, to beat the crap out of my mother's boyfriend."

"Sean—" She snaked an arm around his middle and held him.

He was grateful and tightened his hold on her in response. The years fell away easily and he was back in that miserable apartment in Vegas.

"The air-conditioning was broken, as usual," he said, his voice soft and reluctant, as he mentally went back to a time he wished to hell he could forget. "It was so damn hot, it felt as if every breath I took was setting fire to my lungs."

He paused and said, "Eric, Mom's boyfriend, was a big guy with what you could say was anger-management issues." He smiled tightly at the understatement. "He'd been beating on my mother for a couple of years. She always threw him out, and she always took him back. And I couldn't *do* anything about it."

God, he remembered the frustration, the fury that used to claw at his throat. He'd ached to be big enough that he could finally defend his mother. Take care of her.

And at last, that day came.

"He hit her again on my sixteenth birthday, and I hit him back."

Melinda said nothing, and he didn't look down at her, not wanting to see what was in her face. Pity? Revulsion? Didn't think he could take either one. So he kept his gaze fixed on the wall opposite and let his memories dredge up the images.

"He went down, and I think I was as surprised as he was," Sean admitted. And through the prism of time, he remembered seeing the bastard stare up at him out of eyes glittering with fury and fear.

"But like most bullies, he didn't like being hit as much

as he enjoyed being the one doing the hitting. So he just laid there on the floor, staring up at me like I had grown two heads.

"Mom was there too, and her latest black eye was just starting to bloom on her face." He laughed shortly. "I was so damn proud of myself that I looked to her expecting to see a little hero worship."

"What happened?" Melinda whispered.

Sean took a breath and said flatly, "She dropped to her knees beside Eric and shouted at me to get out."

"*What*?"

He smiled a little at the outrage in her voice, but he still didn't turn his gaze on her. Didn't quite trust himself to finish this sordid little tale if he was looking at Melinda.

"Eric pushed away from her and headed out the front door, cursing and stumbling a little, which I admit, made me feel good in spite of everything. Mom chased after him," Sean added. "But before she left she told me to leave and that she never wanted to see me again."

"She was wrong," Melinda said, pulling out of his grip to turn and look at him.

He couldn't avoid staring into her eyes, and he noticed the fierce, righteous indignation shining in those blue depths. She was infuriated on his behalf, and Sean appreciated it. But the story was old and long since over.

"Doesn't matter anymore," he assured her, though the dark spot in a corner of his heart still burned with the memory.

Even now, so many years later, he could remember the look on his mother's face. And just like every time the memory sneaked up on him, he tried to put a name to the expression she wore as she looked at him. Disgust? Fury? *Hatred*? The last bruise on her cheek was a mass of green and yellow streaks, visible even beneath her carefully applied makeup. And still, she had defended the bastard.

In his mind, Sean could hear her voice.

"He loved me. He took care of me. You had no right. You're just like your father, out for yourself and screw everybody else."

"Where did you go?" Melinda's voice again, tearing him from the past and grounding him in the present.

He leaned his head back against the bed. "I called my dad. He sent a King jet for me, and I went to live with him."

"Well thank God for your father, anyway."

Sean chuckled. "Not too many people have ever said that about Ben King."

"Well I am. Your mom was wrong, Sean."

"Maybe. But because of what I did, I never saw her again," he said, his gaze locked on hers. "She died a few years later."

"Did Eric—"

"No," he answered quickly. "Car accident on the strip. Some tourist ran her down one night."

"I'm sorry, Sean. So sorry." Her features were a mask of sympathy and fury for what he'd gone through. But Melinda wasn't finished. "You shouldn't feel guilty about what you did. It was right."

He looked at her then and saw the fierceness in her eyes. All directed at easing his pain, and something inside him tightened another notch. She was the first person, other than his brothers, to care about what he was feeling. To try to make it better. Warmth stole through him, and Sean realized that talking about the past had actually distanced him from it as he had never been able to do before. He felt…freer than he had in a very long time.

He was walking a thinner and thinner line every damn

day with Melinda. He knew it. He felt it. But damned if he could pull away.

"And you shouldn't feel guilty about today," he said quietly. "It's okay to be alive, you know."

She stroked her fingertips along his cheek with a featherlight touch. He caught her hand and turned his face to plant a kiss in the center of her palm. "Let go of the guilt, Melinda. Trust me when I say holding onto it will tear you apart."

As he watched, she glanced down at the photo she still held in one hand. Sean looked at the framed picture too and knew without a doubt that he hated Steven Hardesty. And no way would he let her turn her back on a life for the sake of a dead man.

Deliberately, he took the picture from her and set it facedown on the bedside table. "Steven's gone, Melinda."

She took a long, shuddering breath and let it out again. "I know."

"Would he want you to be miserable forever?"

"No."

"Then let him go. Be with me." He tipped her chin up so her eyes, red-rimmed from crying and pain, were focused on him. "I'm safe, Melinda. I'm the rebound guy. I'm temporary." His fingers smoothed away the last of her tears, and he leaned in to kiss her forehead. "Use me to heal your heart, Melinda. I won't be here long. We both know that. There's no complications here. I don't want anything from you."

Okay, yes, he was being a little self-serving, he told himself. Because he did want Melinda more than his next gulp of air. But it was also true. He wouldn't be staying with her. And if he could get her past wanting to bury herself, then they would both be able to walk away a little easier when their time together was done.

A wistful smile lifted one corner of her mouth, and he took his first easy breath since entering this room.

"I didn't mean to have a meltdown," she said.

"It's okay—"

"No, it's not," she said firmly. "I was fine, really. I came up here and I was going to shower and wait for you when I saw—" Her voice trailed off as she glanced at the face-down photo. "And suddenly, it all hit me. He's gone. I'm here. With you. And I felt *bad* because I was feeling so *good*. And that doesn't make any sense at all, does it?"

"You're wrong about that, too. It makes perfect sense." Sean brushed her hair back from her face and felt a gentle warmth slide through him as he pulled her in and held her. This wasn't the heat he felt when he touched her. This was something more. Something deeper. Something he couldn't describe—and he didn't think he should try.

She leaned into him, and his arms just naturally tightened around her.

"Big day, huh?" she whispered.

"Yeah. You tired?" he asked.

She looked up at him and shook her head.

He smiled. "Glad to hear it."

When he kissed her, Melinda melted against him, giving herself up to the truth of the moment. She was alive, as Sean had said, and she wasn't going to hide from life again. She was going to set guilt aside and reach for what she wanted.

And what she wanted was Sean.

In a few seconds, they were naked. Sean grabbed a condom, sheathed himself, then sprawled across her bed with her. She felt the delicious slide of Sean's skin against hers. He kissed his way down her body, lips and tongue tracing fiery lines across her flesh. He suckled at her breasts until she was arching blindly beneath him, desperate to ease the coiled tension inside her.

But there was more. He didn't stop. Whispered words became muffled as he continued to gently torture her. Her breath was labored and she stared up at the ceiling, losing herself in the sensations that only he could cause.

His hands explored her every curve, his mouth tasted every inch of her, and when he moved down, kissing his way past her abdomen, she tensed. He spread her legs and kneeled between them, scooping his hands beneath her to lift her hips off the bed.

"Sean…"

"Just enjoy," he said and covered her core with his mouth.

She gasped and moved into him, loving the feel of his tongue on her most sensitive skin. Again and again, he licked and nibbled at her center, until she was wild with need. With banked passion spilling up and over, inside her.

Her first climax hit her hard, and she called his name brokenly as her body quivered and shook and then finally exploded into shiny shards of pleasure. She was still quaking with release when his body slid into hers, pushing her into another orgasm, even more profound than the one before.

She reached for him, locking her feet at the small of his back, holding him to her, taking him deeper. Her hips rocked with his in a rhythm that was both breathless and timeless. Their bodies moved as one. Melinda looked up into his eyes and fell into those blue depths that were so filled with old pain and new promise.

He kissed her, and she took him inside, tangling her tongue with his. When he broke the kiss and smiled down at her, she smiled back, feeling freer than she ever had. Happiness dropped down on top of her, and she hardly recognized it. He had done this, she thought wildly. He had opened her heart, her body, her life.

That last, improbable thought dissolved an instant later when her body reached its peak and she gave herself up to the overwhelming crash of something amazing. She held onto him and cried out his name as she broke apart again, safe in his arms.

She held onto him as his body joined hers and, together, they slid into oblivion.

In the quiet, Melinda realized that she cared for Sean, far more than she should. But it wasn't love.

Couldn't be.

Because if it was, she had set herself up for even more heartbreak.

Two days later, Sean stood up from his desk and turned to look out his office window. Couldn't keep his mind on work. Couldn't really think about anything but Melinda and this mess he'd landed them both in.

He'd thought to seduce her. Hadn't really planned on his *own* reaction to the plan. Funny, he had once warned his brother Lucas to pull back from his idiotic idea to use Rose Clancy as a means of revenge against her brother Dave. Sean could remember telling Lucas that his plan was going to turn on him. And damned if it didn't. Although, that had all worked out in the end, since Lucas and Rose were happily married now—not to mention the parents of the cutest three-month-old boy in the world.

"Should've listened to your own advice," he muttered, disgusted with himself. But no, true to King form, he'd figured he could handle his own life just fine. Now, he was stuck in the middle of a damn soap opera.

A marriage of convenience to a woman still mourning the death of her once fiancé—and getting deeper and deeper into…what? Lust? *Love*?

That thought backed him right up. It hit him hard, and he shook his head as if he could wipe away even the silent mention of the word. He wasn't in love. He didn't do love. He'd tried that once only to get kicked in the teeth for his trouble.

"No, not love. Serious *like*, maybe," he hedged and winced at the idiocy of that statement.

He really hated to admit that his brothers had been right. He never should have married Melinda. It had been asking for trouble right from the jump, and it was only getting worse the longer this marriage lasted. Even if he wasn't in love, he was definitely feeling something for Melinda. Something that had him worried enough that he wondered how the hell he was supposed to deal with this for the next several weeks. He'd already decided that he would go out of his way to not have to come back to Tesoro during the length of the construction job.

Once he was gone from the island, he was going to stay gone. No sense putting him or Melinda through unnecessarily awkward situations. But damned if he wanted to think about leaving, either.

Sean stared out the window and realized that though he had only been on Tesoro a couple of weeks, he'd already become accustomed to the view here.

At first, it had all been foreign to him. Every time he looked out a window, he expected to see Long Beach. Busy streets, tons of people and his favorite Mexican restaurant on the corner. He had felt out of place, and he'd missed his water tower home and the familiar feel of Sunset Beach.

But now, looking out over clear blue water, white beaches and seeing only the occasional car felt…right.

Somehow, the island had sneaked into his system. Much like Melinda had, he admitted silently.

This place, this woman, were becoming more important to him every day. Yet he knew he couldn't afford to get attached to either one of them since he would be leaving in a few short weeks.

His brain was running in circles. He wasn't finding answers to any of his questions—only more questions. Which gave him a damn headache and had him reaching for his phone gratefully when it rang.

A glance at the caller ID had him smiling. "Garrett."

"Sean, got some news for you."

"Right." He focused on his cousin's voice and pushed thoughts of Melinda to one side for the moment. God knew there'd be plenty of time later to deal with the ramifications of this temporary marriage. "What'd you find out?"

"Mainly?" Garret asked. "I found out Steven Hardesty was a creep."

Sean inhaled sharply and nodded as his gut feeling was vindicated.

"Not surprised," he said. "You should see his picture. No one with that many teeth is a good guy."

"Yeah." Garrett snorted. "Anyway, seems our Mr. Hardesty was a small-time con. Used his charm to bilk women out of money, then he'd disappear. There are a couple of police departments in Europe who'd love to have a chat with him."

"Tough to manage, him being dead and all," Sean muttered.

"Yeah, I actually told them about his death. They were disappointed."

Thinking about Melinda mourning this guy, crying because she'd felt she was cheating on him with Sean, just made Sean's stomach churn and his temper spike. "So he was a thief."

"Oh yeah, and from what I can tell, he had moved up to embezzling just before his untimely passing."

"Embezzling?" Sean's spine went stiff as a board. His gaze was fixed on the harbor, but he hardly noticed the panorama stretched out in front of him. "From who?"

"Walter Stanford."

"Damn it." Sean's hand fisted on his phone tightly enough that he wouldn't have been surprised to snap the plastic case. Not only was the late, great Steven setting Melinda up to be used, and to no doubt drain her trust fund, but he had been stealing from the old man, too?

Quietly furious, Sean couldn't help wondering if this was why Walter's finances were in such bad shape. If Steven had been siphoning money from the hotel…" You sure about this?"

"Oh yeah. There's enough of a paper trail to prove it."

"Good." Not that Sean had any imminent plans to tell Melinda about this, but he was sure as hell going to tell Walter. And it was good to know there was proof if the old man needed it.

"Sounds like your Melinda got off easy with this guy dying before he could cheat her and leave her."

"Sounds that way, doesn't it." Garrett was clearly as disgusted as Sean. "Thanks Garrett. Appreciate it."

"No problem, cuz. Call if you need anything else."

When he hung up, Sean thought about Garrett's statement. If Steven hadn't died, Melinda would have been hurt and betrayed. She probably would have lost the money she was counting on to make her independent. But more, she'd have felt foolish and might have gone on a man-hating spree. But as it stood, she didn't know the guy was a creep. To her, he was still the beloved fiancé, so instead of being pissed off, she was dealing with survivor's guilt.

Steven Hardesty didn't deserve one of Melinda's tears. Tossing the phone onto his desk, Sean turned to the window again. He threw it open, allowing the ocean wind to rush in at him. The scent of the sea and the cool air didn't do a damn thing to settle his mind. Bottom line? He didn't know what the hell to do with this knowledge.

Should he tell Melinda? If she believed him, it would break her heart. If she didn't believe him, she'd hate Sean for trying to destroy her memory of Steven.

"Hell, even dead, the bastard is winning."

Riding a wave of banked fury, Sean knew there was one person at least, who should be told the truth. He pushed away from the window, stalked across the room and left, slamming the door behind him.

Eleven

For the first time, Walter Stanford looked old.

Sean swallowed back his own anger and sense of righteous indignation and focused on the man sitting at his desk.

Walter stared down at his empty hands as if accusing them of being helpless. Shaking his head slowly, he took several long, deep breaths before speaking in a soft voice filled with regret and just a hint of the fury Sean was still feeling.

"Yes, I knew about Steven's theft. He had been here for little more than year," Walter said, lifting his gaze to meet Sean's. "And in that time, he managed to feather quite a nice nest for himself—at my expense."

"So he *is* the reason the hotel is having hard times."

"Not entirely," Walter said with a tired sigh. "Truthfully, I made a few bad investments and, in all honesty, should have opened the island to more tourism. Not just for my sake, but for everyone else here. So it wasn't all Steven's fault, though he certainly did his share." Walter picked up a pen, twirled it in his fingers for a second, then tossed it to his desktop in disgust. "Steven must have gotten wind that I was to have him arrested. He was killed when he was driving to the harbor to catch a boat to St. Thomas."

"And you didn't tell Melinda." It wasn't a question.

He fixed his gaze on Sean. "No. Melinda was never aware of my troubles or Steven's perfidy. If he had lived, she would have had to know. As it is, I thought it better to keep my silence."

"Why?" Sean demanded, dropping both hands onto the edge of the desk and leaning in. "Damn it Walter, Melinda's smart. Capable. She doesn't need to be treated like a child."

"Do you think I don't know that?" Walter's anger began to crackle in the room, and it collided with Sean's in a nearly visible shower of sparks. Pushing up from his chair, Walter muttered, "Do you think I enjoy seeing my girl mourning that fraud? Grieving for a cheat of a man who would have left her broken had he been given the chance?"

Sean leaned one hip against the edge of the desk, crossed his arms over his chest and asked a simple question. "Why then? Why keep quiet?"

Walter turned and fixed a hard look on him.

"You're letting her suffer by feeling she's betraying that son-of-a-bitch's memory."

"And you think it would be better if I tell her that he *never* cared for her? That he wanted her only for the money?" Walter snapped the words out in another burst of rage, but a moment later, he looked defeated again. "There is no right answer here," he whispered. "If I don't tell her, she'll torture herself, and if I do tell her, she'll be crushed. How can I know what to do?"

Sean could see the old man's problem. After all, he'd asked himself pretty much the same questions after he had talked to Garrett. But at the same time, it irritated the hell out of him to remember Melinda's tears over the thief who'd died before he could be prosecuted. Still, how could he argue with the man's need to protect his family? Hadn't Sean lost everything at sixteen trying to do the same thing for his mother?

"Could you look into her eyes and tell her?" Walter asked quietly.

He wanted to say yes. Damn it, he didn't want her grieving over Steven one more damn minute. But as he thought about it, the truth was... "No."

At the end, no matter what else was at stake, Sean simply didn't want to be the one to hurt her.

Two days later, Melinda was nervous.

The Kings were arriving to check out the island—and *her*— she thought.

"Relax," he told her as they stood at the dock waiting for the boat from St. Thomas to arrive. "You'll like them all, I promise."

"But they know about our deal, right? So they know we're not your average married couple."

"They know, but it won't matter to them. They're going to love you. So relax."

She nodded and kept staring out at the water. The launch should be here any second. "Tell me again."

He smiled and draped one arm around her shoulder. "Rafe is married to Katie."

"The cookie queen," Melinda added.

"Yep. And Lucas is married to Rose."

"The great cook," she provided. Honestly, she'd heard so much about his brothers and their wives, Melinda had quite the confidence crisis going on. Sean's sisters-in-law sounded brilliant, successful and, most importantly, *loved*.

"And I'm married to the artist," Sean said, dropping a kiss on top of her head.

He said that so lightly. As if they were *really* married and just for a moment, she let herself wonder what that would be like. She glanced up at him and briefly studied his profile as he watched for the approaching boat. His features were sharp and clean. His hair windblown, as she liked it best, and his eyes were hidden behind a pair of dark glasses. He wore a dark red, collared knit shirt and a pair of tan cargoes with his scuffed and battered boots. An anticipatory smile curved his mouth.

And she knew. In a blink. In a heart-stopping, soul-jarring instant, that she *loved* Sean King.

Melinda swayed with the impact of that knowledge and waited for an accompanying stab of guilt to jolt her. But it didn't come. Had she finally, and at last, let Steven's memory go? Was she ready now to love someone else, just in time to say goodbye to him?

"Hey?" Sean tipped his sunglasses down and looked at her over the edge. "You okay? You look a little pale all of a sudden."

Not surprising, she thought, but didn't say. Taking a deep breath she nodded and forced a smile. "I'm fine. Just a little nervous I guess."

Nervous?

Terrified.

He hugged her, drawing her in and giving her a hard squeeze. Then he bent his head, claimed a quick kiss and said, "Don't be. It'll be great. We'll show them the hotel site, go to dinner, have some laughs and they'll go home."

"Right. Back to California," she said, thinking that in just a few more weeks, Sean would be gone too. He'd be back there with his family and she would be here. On Tesoro.

Alone.

"No more time for nerves. They're here."

It was only then that Melinda heard the roar of an engine headed their way. She looked out and saw the Tesoro launch headed into dock.

"Oh, please," Katie said, "my kitchen was perfect. I *paid* you to remodel it and then what did you do?" She didn't wait for an answer, just turned to Melinda and said, "The minute we got married, he decided to renovate the whole house, so he took out the wall!"

"It'll be bigger and feed right into the new family room," Rafe argued with a grin.

"Told you," Sean whispered to Melinda.

"With a home theatre surround sound system," Rafe put in, a gleam in his eye.

"Oh God," Sean said, horrified. "He's not going to make us watch those outer space movies he loves on a big screen, is he?"

"Not me, he's not," Lucas said and jiggled his infant son on his shoulder. "I'm home nights on diaper duty."

Melinda watched them all as the banter flew around the table. They were in a private dining room at the Stanford hotel and the conversation hadn't lagged once since the Kings' arrival two hours before.

Sitting beside Sean on the red leather booth seat, she watched the interaction of the family and found herself envious of the easy solidarity they shared. Seeing Sean with his brothers and their wives showed her yet another side to the man she'd married. There was real affection beneath the teasing, and the warmth she felt from all of them was welcoming.

She really liked Katie and Rose, too. She had been prepared to be intimidated or even feel like a stranger around them. But both women were warm and friendly and seemed to have their King husbands wrapped around their fingers. It was amazing to watch, really. They were all so…connected.

"Oh wow," Katie said suddenly, reaching out to lift Melinda's left hand for a better look. "That's a gorgeous ring!" She flashed Sean a smile. "Nice job on picking it out. Where did you get it? I think Rose and I need to go shopping."

"Actually," Sean said, giving Melinda's shoulders a squeeze, "My clever wife made it."

"She *made* her own wedding ring?" Rose said, sounding appalled.

"Damn, you're cheap," Rafe muttered with a shake of his head.

"Funny," Sean told him. "No, I bought the ring at a jewelry store in town. Later on I found out that Melinda designed and made it herself."

"That's amazing," Rose said, getting a good look at it herself. She lifted her gaze and smiled. "Do you have more?"

"Sure," Melinda said, basking in the praise. "My workshop is here in the hotel."

"Oh boy." Katie wriggled in excitement. "And I'm guessing family gets a private look at all of the sparklies?"

"Sure," Melinda told her, laughing. "We can go now if you want."

"Absolutely," Rose said and scooped her son out of his father's arms. "You guys be good. We're going to spend a lot of money."

"And my son is going why?" Lucas asked with a laugh.

"Never too early to teach him how to shop!" Rose bent down, kissed Lucas, then waited for Katie and Melinda.

Katie kissed Rafe, and Melinda was just scooting out of the booth when Sean pulled her in for a quick, hard kiss. She felt flustered but pleased that he'd kissed her as easily as his brothers had their own wives as she led the women off to the elevators.

"Okay," Rafe asked once the women were out of earshot. "What exactly is going on?"

"What do you mean?" Sean picked up his beer and took a sip, stalling.

"Pitiful." Lucas laughed and took a drink of his beer. "You know exactly what he means. You just don't want to talk about it."

"And since you know that, you'll drop it, right?" Sean slid a glance at him.

"Uh, *no*," Rafe told him before Lucas could speak up. "You told us you were getting married as part of a land deal. Yet, when we get here, we find you all googly-eyed over your new wife."

Well, that was unsettling. Sean frowned at him. "So?"

"*So*," Lucas said, "it doesn't exactly look like a business deal to us."

"That's what it is," Sean muttered. All it could be, he told himself. He and Melinda had made a bargain, and he would stick to it. He never went back on his word.

Besides, as he kept reminding himself, he had already tried marriage and it hadn't exactly been a vacation. The reason this marriage was working was probably because they both knew it was going to end. No pressure. No promises to be kept or vows to take seriously. He nodded to himself and repeated, "It's strictly business."

"Yeah," Lucas said with a snort. "I can see that."

Sean glared at him. "Nobody asked you for your opinion."

"Yeah, because that's how we do things in the King family. We wait to be asked."

"Pay no attention to him," Rafe said, staring at Sean. "Just tell me what's going on. From what I can see, there's more to this marriage than you said there was."

Sean blew out a breath. The dining room was large, but quiet. Since they had the place to themselves, there was no reason not to discuss it. But he didn't like it. For some reason, he felt disloyal to Melinda for talking to his brothers about what was between them. Still, he'd always been able to count on his family. Maybe talking to them would help him straighten things out in his mind.

Because, God knew, a little clarity would come in handy.

"Okay," he said with a nod, "I admit that things aren't quite as clear as they should be."

"You think?" Lucas prompted.

Rafe glared him into silence.

"Fine. I'm not ready to leave her, even though I should be. It doesn't make any sense to me," he muttered, peeling the local label off his beer bottle.

"Brother, you're hooked. Just give in now. Don't fight it." Lucas gave him a slap on the shoulder in solidarity.

"No," Sean argued, looking from one brother to the other. "You don't get it. I'm not husband material." He couldn't believe he was going to do this, Sean thought. But they had to understand. Had to see where he was coming from and why he knew he couldn't be married. "I've tried it before. It didn't work out."

"What?" Rafe and Lucas spoke at the same time, exchanged a look of astonishment, then turned back to Sean. Rafe said, "What're you talking about?"

"I was married once. Never told you guys."

"Why the hell not?" Lucas demanded.

"Because I felt like a jackass, okay?" Sean snapped. "Why would I tell you two that I let some woman…" He stopped and took a deep breath.

"Well, now you have to tell us," Rafe said.

So he did, but he kept it short. "Okay. Her name was Tracy. We met in college. Freshman year. Dated awhile then broke up." Sean paused for a sip of beer and the cold liquid did nothing to ease the dryness in his throat. But he was in this far, he might as well finish it. "Eight months later, she showed up, pregnant. She cried and said how she hadn't wanted to worry me, but she got scared."

"Damn it," Rafe muttered.

"Yeah." Sean smiled wryly. "No way was I going to be the kind of father our dad was, so I married her."

"And?" Lucas asked.

Sean shrugged and realized that telling this story wasn't as terrible as he had imagined. It actually felt good to get it out there. To finally tell his brothers what he'd been hiding for years.

"The baby was a week or two old when Tracy told me he wasn't mine. Seems Tracy's first boyfriend had come back to town. He was the father. She left that day, haven't seen her or the baby since."

"Well hell."

Sean gave Lucas a nod of appreciation. "That about sums it up."

"You should have told us," Rafe said quietly.

Sean shook his head. "No man wants to look like a fool."

"You're only a fool if you didn't learn something," Rafe countered.

"That's the funny part. I thought I had," Sean acknowledged. "Steer clear of marriage. That was the lesson."

"No it wasn't, you idiot," Lucas snapped.

"Hey."

"Shut up, Lucas," Rafe said, never taking his gaze off Sean. "The lesson was to trust yourself. You didn't want to marry Tracy. Hell, you broke up with her."

"Well, yeah, but—"

"No buts," Rafe said with a shake of his head. "The lesson is to trust what you feel, Sean. You felt nothing for Tracy but obligation. If what you're feeling for Melinda is real, and you leave her anyway because of a stupid deal you made, *then* you're a bigger fool than any of us knew."

While his brothers talked, Sean sat in silence and really thought about what Rafe had said. Maybe, and Sean hated to admit it, even privately, his brother was right. For years, the memory of his ex had bothered him. Angered him. Now, he realized, he felt...nothing. Was being with Melinda what had prompted the change?

His mind raced with possibilities.

Melinda had sneaked into his heart. He hadn't seen it coming. But the question was, what did he do about it now?

Katie and Rose bought rings, necklaces, bracelets and earrings. Their good-natured bickering over who got to buy what had Melinda laughing along with them. But their admiration for her work filled her heart and fed her soul. She had never had the opportunity to actually see people's reactions to her stuff before. Well, her friend Kathy loved the jewelry, but she was probably prejudiced by her affection for Melinda. And yes, Melinda did sell a lot of pieces through James's shop, but this was the first time she was able to really *see* that her work was good. Good enough that Rose and Katie bought up most of Melinda's inventory.

"You're very talented," Katie said with a sigh as she admired the Tesoro Topaz glittering on her wrist.

"I agree." Rose cooed at her son as he drank his bottle, but then she looked at Melinda and said, "I know women back home who would pay a fortune for your work."

Back home. Sean's home. Far away from Tesoro and Melinda. An ache settled in the center of her chest, and she absently rubbed it, hoping to ease the pain. It didn't help. God, how had this all gone so wrong?

She'd allowed herself to get involved. To want. To need. To *love*.

And now it was too late to back away. She couldn't tear Sean out of her heart any more than she once could have Steven.

Steven. For just one moment, she thought about the man she had once promised to love forever and wondered how she could have gotten to this place so soon after his death. The guilt that always surrounded thoughts of her late fiancé gathered in close, but she held them at bay.

She couldn't hide from her own emotions anymore. The truth was, she loved Sean so much more deeply than she had ever loved Steven. More passionately. More completely. Melinda hadn't even known she was capable of a love this all-encompassing.

Sean had been right. She couldn't stop living.

But what would he say if he knew that she had ruined their bargain by falling in love with him? Would he run back to California? Would he laugh and tell her she was being silly? Would he panic?

"You love him, don't you?"

"What?" Melinda jolted and looked up at Katie.

"Sean," the woman said. "You're in love with Sean."

Brushing that away, she forced a laugh and busied herself with putting the rest of her finished pieces back in the glass case. "Don't be ridiculous."

"Nope, she's right," Rose said. "It's all over your face, sweetie. Trust me when I say I *know* that look."

Melinda's gaze moved from one to the other of the women and she sighed miserably at their matching expressions of sympathy. "I can't be in love with him. You know about our marriage. The... deal we made."

"Yeah, Rafe and Lucas told us," Katie said.

"But the deal changed, didn't it?" Rose lifted Danny to her shoulder and began patting his back.

Melinda could lie, but she wasn't very good at it. And even as she considered it, she told herself there was no point in trying to deny the truth to these two. They were too smart to believe it, anyway.

"Yes, it changed. For me, at least."

"Look," Katie said quietly, "King men aren't the easiest males in the universe, but they're worth the trouble."

"Absolutely," Rose echoed.

"But you're the only one who can decide if you're willing to fight for him. Because you're going to have to batter down all the walls he's put up around his heart."

"I always thought there was a loneliness about Sean," Rose said thoughtfully, then smiled when the baby burped. "What a good boy."

"I know what you mean," Katie agreed, taking the empty baby bottle from Rose. She capped it and tucked it back into the diaper bag. "He's sweet and funny, yet he always seems to sort of be on the outside, you know?"

Melinda listened and thought about the things Sean had told her about his early life. About the mother who hadn't appreciated the son who tried to protect her. About how he must have felt—thrown aside, forgotten. And yes, she could understand his underlying loneliness. But that didn't mean—

"He needs you, Melinda." Katie nodded as if emphasizing her words. "You love him. Sean needs that."

"Plus," Rose said slyly, "we Wives-of-Kings have to stick together, right?"

"Amen." Katie laughed a little. "I love Rafe like crazy, but King men are the most stubborn, bossy males on the face of the planet."

"Tell me about it," Rose murmured, rocking Danny as he fell asleep. "Did you know, Lucas got rid of my car? Said it wasn't safe."

"The skillet car?" Melinda asked, then explained, "Sean told me about it. I thought it sounded great."

"Thank you, but I kept the skillet." She grinned. "He bought me some monster SUV, said it was safer to drive the baby around in. But I insisted that my skillet go back on top." She laughed in memory. "It almost killed him to put my skillet on top of a new car. But it's there."

"See, Melinda," Katie urged, "they're stubborn but they come around. And believe me, there is no better husband in the world than one of the Kings."

"You don't have to convince me," Melinda assured them both. "I already know how great Sean is. But our marriage is different. We didn't get married for love."

"You said yourself," Katie reminded her, "things change."

Were they right? Could she risk finding out?
Could she live with herself if she *didn't*?

Twelve

A few days later, the King family was gone, with the promise to return soon. The cargo ship had arrived, carrying all of the King company equipment they would need. The crews would be flying into the islands the following week. Time was passing so quickly, Melinda's head spun. Soon, Sean would be leaving—unless she could convince him to stay.

She watched him as he walked the construction site, his gaze taking in everything. As soon as the King crew arrived, they'd begin work on the hotel. For now, Tomin and his sons had the foundation area taped off. Small wooden stakes had been hammered into the ground with white string drawn between them. She could see it now, the footprint of the King hotel and it was immense. It looked at the moment, as empty as she felt. To distract herself from the ache in her heart, she spoke up.

"What were you arguing about with Rafe this morning?"

"Huh?" He stopped walking and looked at her. "What?"

"You and Rafe. I saw the two of you arguing just before they got in the launch to leave."

"Nothing," he said, shaking his head. "It was nothing. Just my brother poking his nose in again. Like always."

"I think it would be wonderful to have family like that. People who care enough about you to get into your business."

He snorted. "Sounds good in theory."

Something was wrong, she'd been feeling it ever since his family left. "Sean, what's going on? You seem a little... tense."

"No. Just thinking."

"About?"

"A lot of things." He pushed one hand through his hair. "Mostly, at the moment, my annoying brother."

She smiled at the irritation in his voice. "What did he say?"

"Oh, he's full of advice, Rafe is," Sean told her wryly. "Not so good at taking it, but excellent at dishing it out."

"You want to tell me about it?"

He laughed, but there was no humor in it, and Melinda's heart gave a little lurch. "That's the question, isn't it? Do I tell you or not?"

Irritation blossomed just beneath the hurt, and she welcomed it. Better to be angry than in pain. "I'd rather know, whatever it is."

Sean looked at her as if trying to decide what to do, and his blue eyes were shadowed with emotions she couldn't read. "I don't like secrets."

"Neither do I."

"Yeah," he muttered. "We'll see."

Then he started talking. He told her about his first marriage and with every word he spoke, Melinda's heart broke a little for him. To be used that way. To have something and then have it ripped away. She felt the old pain in his voice and read the carefully banked emotions in his eyes.

"I'm sorry," she said when he was finished.

He bent down, picked up a rock and threw it. After a second or two, it clattered against more rocks some distance away. Then he walked toward her, closing the distance between them in a few long strides. He wore faded jeans, a dark blue Henley and the boots she was becoming way too fond of. But the look on his face was dark. Haunted.

Instinctively, Melinda reached out to hug him. Wrapping her arms around him, she held on tightly. He didn't respond at first, and that tore at her. But she held on, and, after a moment or two, he returned the embrace, resting his chin on top of her head.

"I'm sorry she hurt you."

"It was a long time ago. She doesn't matter anymore."

Melinda pulled back and looked up at him. "I can't believe you didn't know she was lying."

"Good liars are hard to spot." He stepped back from her.

"I suppose, but no one's ever lied to me like that."

"Oh, Melinda…" He shook his head, snorted a laugh and turned his gaze from hers. "If you knew."

"What?"

"Nothing." His jaw was clenched tight as if he were holding back a flood of words clamoring to get out. "Never mind."

"Oh no," she countered, taking his arm and holding on. "If you have something to say to me, say it."

"There's no point."

"What are you talking about?"

He stepped away from her, shoved both hands into his back pockets and propped one boot on a rock beside him. "Melinda, I'm in a piss-poor mood. Now's not the time. Let's just go, and forget all about this."

"No," she repeated. "There's something you want to say, so say it, Sean. It's been eating at you all day. Do you think I can't see it? Tell me."

He studied her for a long minute, then seemed to come to a decision. "Fine. You said you'd rather know the truth than have secrets?"

"Yes." Warning bells were going off inside her, but she didn't listen. Everything in her braced for whatever was coming and still, she was unprepared.

"Okay." He rubbed the back of his neck, locked eyes with her and said, "I'm not the only one who can't spot a liar. You didn't notice that your beloved Steven was robbing your grandfather blind."

"What?" She staggered back a step, shock draining the blood from her brain until she felt almost light-headed.

He gave a short, harsh laugh. "Yeah, the wonderful Steven was a con man with dozens of poorer but wiser women in his background."

"You're lying," she whispered as a cold, tight band wrapped itself around her chest. She couldn't breathe. Spots danced in her vision, and she shook her head to clear it.

"I don't lie." He held up one hand. "Wait. I guess I do. Because I've known about that jackass fiancé of yours for days and didn't say anything."

"How? Why?"

"I had my cousin Garrett do some checking into Steven's background. Wasn't hard to find." He pulled his hands from his pockets and rubbed them both over his face as if he could somehow wipe away this whole afternoon.

It didn't work though, and Sean was forced to watch her as the truth slammed home. He should have kept quiet. Damn Rafe and his advice to tell Melinda the truth. To let her know what kind of man Steven was so that she'd be ready to take a chance—a *real* chance—with Sean.

Why in the hell would she want to be with the man who had shattered her nice, pretty world? God, he was an idiot for listening to his brother. Rafe had advised coming clean. Telling Melinda about what Garrett had discovered—but mainly, confessing to her that he loved her. But he didn't see the second half of that plan happening now. And the minute he got back to Long Beach, he would punch Rafe dead in the face as a big thank you.

But for now, he was standing opposite the woman he loved and watching as he slowly destroyed everything she had believed in.

"You're wrong. Steven wouldn't do that. He wouldn't steal from my grandfather."

"Damn it, Melinda!" Frustration bubbled over, and there was no stopping what he said next. "See the truth! He was a thief and a liar. He was planning on taking your money and dumping you. He'd already stolen from your grandfather and would have been arrested that last day but he died first, the bastard."

Her mouth fell open and a single tear slid from the corner of her right eye. Sean tracked its progress, along her cheek, like a sunlit diamond. She didn't wipe it away and no more followed.

"My grandfather knew?"

"Yes."

"He never said...."

"He didn't want to hurt you."

"So he *lied* to me too?"

"To protect you," he muttered and wished he could call this whole conversation back. He'd been feeling tension mount all day and that last-minute fight with Rafe hadn't helped anything.

But time was passing. The crews would be arriving soon. Melinda had her trust fund, it had been wired into her account on St. Thomas. Soon, he'd be leaving, and that knowledge had been eating at him for too long.

"I shouldn't have said anything," he muttered, disgusted with himself, the situation, but mostly, with Steven.

"You're sorry you told me."

"Yeah."

"Because I need protecting?"

"Well, yeah."

"That is the most insulting thing I've ever heard," she said, words tumbling together. A cold wind shot over the property, buffeted them both, then swept across the island. Waves crashed like a frenzied heartbeat and Melinda looked…pissed.

This was going well.

"I don't need to be protected, Sean. I'm an adult whether you and my grandfather choose to see it or not. I can take hearing the truth no matter how hard it gets." She moved in on him, eyes narrowed, mouth grim.

Being a sensible man, Sean took a step back.

She kept coming and poked her index finger into his chest as if she could drill through to the other side. "What you're telling me is that everyone in my life has been *lying* to me. My grandfather. Steven. *You.*"

Fine, she had a right to be mad. But damned if he'd stand for being compared to that dead jackass one more time. "Don't lump us in with that dirtbag," Sean argued hotly. "That SOB was scamming you. We were—"

"Lying to me," she finished for him. "It doesn't matter *why*, Sean. My God, you don't even see it, do you? How could I have thought I was in love with you?"

"What?" Had he heard that right? The open black hole in his chest filled with hope, but a moment later, that hope drained away.

"At least I loved the man I thought you were," she corrected. "But if you've been lying about this, then how do I know you haven't lied about other things?"

"I haven't." He grabbed her shoulders, pulled her close. "Melinda, nothing that happened between us was a lie."

"And I should take your word for that, I suppose?" She looked up into his eyes, and Sean saw not only fury, but pain in those blue depths. Pain that he had caused by dumping all of this on her. Lucas was right. Sean *was* an idiot. He was about to lose the woman he loved, and there wasn't a thing he could do about it. He'd blown this so badly he couldn't see a way out.

"I won't be lied to anymore," she told him, and though her voice was soft the determination in it was unmistakable. "This temporary marriage is over, Sean. We both got what we wanted out of the deal. Now it's done."

A cold fist squeezed his heart. "Melinda…"

"I don't want to talk to you anymore," she said and turned to walk to the car. "Just please take me back to the hotel."

Sean watched her go, and a big piece of his heart went with her.

Sean moved out of their suite as soon as they returned to the hotel. Melinda didn't watch him leave. She didn't think she could stand it. Instead, she went to her grandfather. Her fury with him wasn't as deep as what she felt for Sean. Because her grandfather's actions she could understand. He would always see her as a child. As that small girl she had been when her world dissolved and only *he* had been able to protect her.

But Sean, Melinda told herself for three days, should have known better. He should have told her the truth as soon as he learned it. She had had a right to know that the man she had mourned so deeply wasn't who she thought he was.

Now, she stood at Steven's grave as a cold wind tossed her hair into her eyes. She'd come here to say goodbye, and now she knew it hadn't even been necessary. Steven was the past and she'd already wasted too much time on a man who hadn't deserved it.

Silly to be talking to a headstone, but Melinda needed to say a few things and this was the only way to get it done. "I'm not even mad at you anymore. I'm angrier with myself. See, what I felt for you is nothing compared to what I feel for Sean. But I was in such a hurry to love and be loved, that I let you convince me that what I felt was real. The truth was, we were *both* lying."

She sighed and looked out over the cemetery with its trees, neatly clipped grass and sprinkling of monuments. "You didn't love me, and, as it turns out, I didn't really love you, either."

Melinda knew now what love was. It was the overwhelming emptiness in her heart where Sean used to be. It was knowing that nothing in her world would ever be right again because the most important person in it was gone.

Nodding to herself, she looked back down at Steven's grave and said, "I just had to face you before I can do what I have to do. I'm going to California. I'm going to find Sean and tell him I love him. I'm going to tell him that I was angry, but that I never stopped loving him. And then

I'm going to drag him back to Tesoro. Where he belongs. With me."

Then she walked away and didn't look back.

She had one last piece to finish for James's shop before she could leave the island to face Sean. Melinda bent her head to her task, carefully using the wire wrapping tool to ease the fine gold wire around a flat topaz. She fought for concentration, forcing her mind away from the man she loved to the pendant in front of her. But it wasn't easy.

"And interruptions won't help," she muttered when a knock sounded on her workroom door.

Disgusted, she got up to answer it and found a small man in an elegant suit smiling at her. "Melinda King?"

"Yes," she said, praying that she would be keeping that name.

"Excellent," he said, stepping into the room and sending his gaze darting over everything. "Ah…" He spotted the glass case and walked to it.

It was only half full, since Rose and Katie had purchased so many pieces. But what was there clearly had the little man captivated.

"Beautiful. Even lovelier than the pieces I saw in town."

"Excuse me," Melinda said, leaving the door open— just in case he was crazy—"who are you?"

"Forgive me," he said, whirling around to hand her a business card that read *Fontenot Fine Jewels*. "I'm Dominic Fontenot, and I believe I'm about to make you a very wealthy woman."

"What?" She looked from the card to the man and back again.

"I spoke with your husband, Sean King? He insisted I come to the island to see your work for myself, and I can tell you, I don't ordinarily enjoy travel." He sighed and glanced at the jewelry again. "But this was worth it. I would like to represent your work. I can promise you that a designer of your talent will go far. Why, this necklace alone…" he pointed to the teardrop design Melinda had made for Kathy, "would easily fetch more than twenty thousand dollars."

She staggered a little and slapped one hand down on the glass case to steady herself. "Twenty—"

"Your husband spoke so highly of your talent," the man said, sighing wistfully. "It's very clear to me that he loves you very much."

At least he used to, Melinda told herself sadly. Her heart ached. Sean must have set up this meeting before he left. He had believed in her talent. In her. He'd found a way to help make her dreams come true. And she'd allowed her own hurt and anger to let him slip away. God. She was such an idiot.

"When did you last speak with my husband?"

He checked the gold watch on his left wrist. "Oh, an hour ago."

"What?" Shock jolted her. "Where? I mean, where did you see him?"

The man blinked at her in surprise. "Why, at the hotel not far from here. It's much smaller, but he explained that he was using it as office space. Now, if you'd like to discuss—"

He was *here*? Sean hadn't left Tesoro? Hadn't left *her*? The dark cloud that had been hanging over her heart suddenly shattered under the force of what felt like a million suns exploding inside her. Melinda could hardly breathe.

She smiled, then grinned, then laughed out loud.

"Mrs. King?"

"God, that sounds good," she said, still laughing. "Mrs. King. Mrs. Sean King. Now and forever."

"We were speaking about your work," Mr. Fontenot said slowly and carefully as if he were speaking to a deranged three-year-old.

And Melinda could see why he would think that.

"I'm so sorry," she blurted. "But it'll have to wait. I really do want to talk to you, but first I have to see my husband. I'll be back. Later. Much later, hopefully." She laughed wildly, gave the man a quick hug and said, "I really have to go!"

"Well, go and talk to her!"

Sean gripped the phone more tightly and said, "You know what, Rafe, I'm done taking your advice. I'll go see Melinda when I think it's time."

"Always were a hardhead," his brother muttered.

"Good talking to you, too," Sean snapped and shut the phone off. He tossed it onto his desk and scowled. Three days since he left Melinda. Felt like three years.

The hotel where the King crew would be staying was just a few miles from the Stanford hotel. But as far as what Sean was feeling, it might as well have been on the dark side of the moon. He was further away from Melinda than ever and waiting to see her was slowly killing him.

He rubbed the center of his chest in what was becoming a habit. But the pain that was lodged around his heart just kept throbbing in time with his pulse. She was in his soul. His bones. She was a part of him and until he got her back, nothing was worth a damn.

He kicked the desk and a scatter of papers floated to the floor. "Damn it," he grumbled and bent to pick them up.

"Mr. Fontenot told me where you were."

Sean froze at the sound of that voice. The one voice he'd hungered to hear for days now. Slowly, he stood up and turned to face the woman he loved. Melinda stood in the open doorway, and the world started turning again. Everything in him came back to life in a painful rush. Just seeing her was enough to ease the aching inside him. But he wanted more.

"Thought he might." Sean couldn't stop staring at her. Everything about her was perfect, from her wind-tousled hair to her red T-shirt to her favorite sneakers.

He had hoped that she would come to him after talking with Dominic. But if she hadn't come, Sean would have gone to her by nightfall.

"You didn't leave," she said, taking a single step into the room.

"Of course not."

"Why did you let me think you did?"

"I was giving you time to cool off," he admitted, scraping one hand across the back of his neck.

"How much longer were you going to stay away?"

"Couldn't have waited much longer," he admitted. And now, looking at her, he couldn't imagine how he had waited this long. "If you hadn't come here, I'd have been beating your door down tonight."

Her mouth curved into a faint smile before it was gone again. "I was leaving at the end of the week. Going to Long Beach. To see you."

He drew his first easy breath in way too long. "Yeah?"

"Yeah." She nodded and whispered, "I thought you left me."

Sean stalked across the room and stopped right in front of her. Staring into her eyes, he willed her to believe him when he said, "I *love* you, Melinda. I will *never* leave you."

She gasped and smiled. "You do?"

"Yes."

"But you miss your home. I know that and—"

"You *are* my home," he said simply and caught her when she threw herself into his arms.

"I love you so much," she whispered, and Sean held her tighter, harder, glorying in the sound of those words and grateful as hell that she'd said them.

"Damn, Melinda, I've missed you. Longest three days of my life."

"You've been here?" she whispered, voice muffled against his shoulder. "At Grandfather's other hotel? All this time?"

"Yes," he said, kissing her neck, her jaw, moving his mouth up to take hers in a fierce, hard kiss that left him hungering for more. "And it's been hell."

"I'm so glad."

He laughed. "That's my girl. One of us suffers, we *both* suffer."

"Exactly. Oh, Sean I missed you, too." She drew her head back to look up at him. "I'm so sorry. I told you I wanted the truth and then when you gave it to me, I turned on you."

"I could have told you in an easier way." He cupped her face in his palms.

She sighed and the sound slipped into his heart and twisted there. "I was only angry because you were keeping things from me for 'my own good.'"

"Yeah, and I'm sorry about that, Melinda. It was never about thinking you couldn't deal with the truth. It was more that I didn't want to be the one to hurt you."

"I get it," she said, covering his hands with her own. "But no more secrets, okay?"

"Absolutely." He kissed her again and grinned down at her. "From now on, it's the whole truth. Starting with,

I love you more than life and I'm going to need an extension on our little marriage deal."

She grinned back at him. "Yeah? For how long?"

"I'm thinking, forever."

"Is that all?" she teased as he pulled her into the room and closed the door behind her.

"Forever and two months," he said, tearing his shirt off then helping Melinda take off hers. "Sound about right?"

"Sounds perfect," she said, moving into him, lifting her face for his kiss. "Because since we're all about honesty now, I love you Sean King. More than I ever thought it possible to love anyone. And I am never going to let you out of our marriage bargain."

"Best news I've ever heard," Sean said, holding her so tightly, he could feel the beat of her heart against his own chest. He felt whole for the first time in his life and he had this one amazing woman to thank for it. "Oh, hey. There's something I want to show you."

Reluctantly, he let her go, but kept a tight grip on her hand as he drew her over to his cluttered desk. There were sketches scattered across the surface and he picked up the top one and handed it to her.

"What is it?" She looked up into his eyes, and he felt warmed to his bones by the love shining in her gaze.

"It's our new house," he said. "No more hotel living for us. Rose taught me how to cook a little, but we can hire a chef if neither one of us wants to do all the cooking."

"A house?"

"I want to build it by that cove where we made love the first time." Pointing to a building to one side of the main structure, he said, "That's your new workroom. Lots of natural light. Plenty of space—"

"Sean…" She took a breath and lifted one hand to

cover her mouth as she stared at the sketch. "You did this for me?"

"For us."

"But what about California?" she asked, "I thought you'd want to go home."

He smiled. "No, I already told you. Home for me is where you are, and Tesoro is where you belong."

Tears rolled along her cheeks, but her smile told him just how happy she was. "God, I love you. This house, the workshop, it's all so beautiful."

"It will be, if you're in it," he told her, "because without you, I've got nothing."

Melinda took both of his hands in hers and felt more joy than she had ever known rise up inside her.

"With you," she said, "I've got everything."

He swept her up into his arms to carry her to the bed and Melinda knew there was nowhere else she wanted to be.

* * * * *

PASSION

For a spicier, decidedly hotter read—
this is your destination for romance!

COMING NEXT MONTH
AVAILABLE JANUARY 10, 2012

#2131 TERMS OF ENGAGEMENT
Ann Major

#2132 SEX, LIES AND THE SOUTHERN BELLE
Dynasties: The Kincaids
Kathie DeNosky

#2133 THE NANNY BOMBSHELL
Billionaires and Babies
Michelle Celmer

#2134 A COWBOY COMES HOME
Colorado Cattle Barons
Barbara Dunlop

#2135 INTO HIS PRIVATE DOMAIN
The Men of Wolff Mountain
Janice Maynard

#2136 A SECRET BIRTHRIGHT
Olivia Gates

You can find more information on upcoming Harlequin® titles,
free excerpts and more at www.HarlequinInsideRomance.com.

HDCNM1211

REQUEST YOUR FREE BOOKS!
2 FREE NOVELS PLUS 2 FREE GIFTS!

ALWAYS POWERFUL, PASSIONATE AND PROVOCATIVE

YES! Please send me 2 FREE Harlequin Desire® novels and my 2 FREE gifts (gifts are worth about $10). After receiving them, if I don't wish to receive any more books, I can return the shipping statement marked "cancel." If I don't cancel, I will receive 6 brand-new novels every month and be billed just $4.30 per book in the U.S. or $4.99 per book in Canada. That's a saving of at least 14% off the cover price! It's quite a bargain! Shipping and handling is just 50¢ per book in the U.S. and 75¢ per book in Canada.* I understand that accepting the 2 free books and gifts places me under no obligation to buy anything. I can always return a shipment and cancel at any time. Even if I never buy another book, the two free books and gifts are mine to keep forever.

225/326 HDN FEF3

Name _____ (PLEASE PRINT) _____

Address _____ Apt. # _____

City _____ State/Prov. _____ Zip/Postal Code _____

Signature (if under 18, a parent or guardian must sign)

Mail to the **Reader Service:**
IN U.S.A.: P.O. Box 1867, Buffalo, NY 14240-1867
IN CANADA: P.O. Box 609, Fort Erie, Ontario L2A 5X3

Not valid for current subscribers to Harlequin Desire books.

Want to try two free books from another line?
Call 1-800-873-8635 or visit www.ReaderService.com.

* Terms and prices subject to change without notice. Prices do not include applicable taxes. Sales tax applicable in N.Y. Canadian residents will be charged applicable taxes. Offer not valid in Quebec. This offer is limited to one order per household. All orders subject to credit approval. Credit or debit balances in a customer's account(s) may be offset by any other outstanding balance owed by or to the customer. Please allow 4 to 6 weeks for delivery. Offer available while quantities last.

Your Privacy—The Reader Service is committed to protecting your privacy. Our Privacy Policy is available online at www.ReaderService.com or upon request from the Reader Service.

We make a portion of our mailing list available to reputable third parties that offer products we believe may interest you. If you prefer that we not exchange your name with third parties, or if you wish to clarify or modify your communication preferences, please visit us at www.ReaderService.com/consumerschoice or write to us at Reader Service Preference Service, P.O. Box 9062, Buffalo, NY 14269. Include your complete name and address.

HDES11B

Harlequin Presents®

USA TODAY bestselling author

Penny Jordan

brings you her newest romance

PASSION
AND THE PRINCE

Prince Marco di Lucchesi can't hide his proud
disdain for fiery English rose Lily Wrightington—
or his attraction to her! While touring the palazzos
of northern Italy, the atmosphere heats up...until
shadows from Lily's past come out....

*Can Marco keep his passion under wraps
enough to protect her, or will it unleash itself, too?*

Find out in January 2012!

*Brittany Grayson survived a horrible ordeal at the hands
of a serial killer known as The Professional…
who's after her now?*

*Harlequin® Romantic Suspense presents a new installment
in Carla Cassidy's reader-favorite miniseries,*
LAWMEN OF BLACK ROCK.

Enjoy a sneak peek of
TOOL BELT DEFENDER.

*Available January 2012
from Harlequin® Romantic Suspense.*

"**B**rittany?" His voice was deep and pleasant and made
her realize she'd been staring at him openmouthed through
the screen door.

"Yes, I'm Brittany and you must be…" Her mind suddenly went blank.

"Alex. Alex Crawford, Chad's friend. You called him
about a deck?"

As she unlocked the screen, she realized she wasn't
quite ready yet to allow a stranger inside, especially a male
stranger.

"Yes, I did. It's nice to meet you, Alex. Let's walk around
back and I'll show you what I have in mind," she said. She
frowned as she realized there was no car in her driveway.
"Did you walk here?" she asked.

His eyes were a warm blue that stood out against his
tanned face and was complemented by his slightly shaggy
dark hair. "I live three doors up." He pointed up the street to
the Walker home that had been on the market for a while.

"How long have you lived there?"

"I moved in about six weeks ago," he replied as they

walked around the side of the house.

That explained why she didn't know the Walkers had moved out and Mr. Hard Body had moved in. Six weeks ago she'd still been living at her brother Benjamin's house trying to heal from the trauma she'd lived through.

As they reached the backyard she motioned toward the broken brick patio just outside the back door. "What I'd like is a wooden deck big enough to hold a barbecue pit and an umbrella table and, of course, lots of people."

He nodded and pulled a tape measure from his tool belt. "An outdoor entertainment area," he said.

"Exactly," she replied and watched as he began to walk the site. The last thing Brittany had wanted to think about over the past eight months of her life was men. But looking at Alex Crawford definitely gave her a slight flutter of pure feminine pleasure.

Will Brittany be able to heal in the arms of Alex, her hotter-than-sin handyman...or will a second psychopath silence her forever? Find out in
TOOL BELT DEFENDER
Available January 2012
from Harlequin® Romantic Suspense
wherever books are sold.

HRSEXP0112

SPECIAL EDITION

Life, Love and Family

Karen Templeton

introduces

The FORTUNES *of* TEXAS: Whirlwind Romance

When a tornado destroys Red Rock, Texas,
Christina Hastings finds herself trapped in the
rubble with telecommunications heir
Scott Fortune. He's handsome, smart and
everything Christina has learned to guard herself
against. As they await rescue, an unlikely attraction
forms between the two and Scott soon finds
himself wanting to know about this mysterious
beauty. But can he catch Christina before she runs
away from her true feelings?

FORTUNE'S CINDERELLA

Available December 27th wherever books are sold!

SSE65643